I0817776

The Holes in Everything and Other Stories

Lumberloft Press

Printed in the United States by Lumberloft Press

ISBN 978-1-7345497-0-6

www.lumberloftpress.com

For Renée…the little engine

Table of Contents

Foreword

Early in 2019, the team at Lumberloft Press released a humble little short fiction contest into the wild with a simple, open-ended prompt: *Death from Above.* We welcomed previously unpublished stories of all genres, and we had modest hopes for a handful of dazzling submissions. We had never run a contest before, so this was in part an experiment to see what we might get back in return.

The contest ran for approximately four months. In the first six weeks, we saw a few dozen submissions come in, and we had settled on the assumption that there might be 50 or so stories to read once the submission deadline arrived. Little did we know that something (we still don't know what exactly) propelled this contest into the sightline of many more writers than we'd ever expect to encounter.

The submissions began pouring in, and at first we thought we had triggered a bot farm somewhere that had made a mistake. But as we began to peek into the stories sent our way, it was clear that this prompt had sparked something that showed no signs of stopping. These were real stories, from real writers, and the material was nothing short of incredible.

All told, when the contest submission window concluded, we had received multiples upon multiples more submissions than we had ever expected. We were floored, extremely grateful, and suddenly, overwhelmed. We are, in fact, a boutique publisher. Our experiment was far more successful than we ever imagined, and the result was that we had millions of words to read within the very short time window we had given ourselves.

We took a long time. Some might say too long. Some might be right. Nevertheless, in the end, we uncovered some amazing literary gems, the best of which we finally announced as our winning submissions in early 2020.

And here we are. Per the rules of our contest, we announced both a grand prize winner and fourteen runners-up, all of which would be included in this very publication you are about to read. This compilation is a journey through the minds of some amazingly talented writers, all exploring the same prompt, but with remarkably different approaches from each. The end result is a stunning array of literature that we are extremely proud to share with the world.

We thank all of the great authors who participated in the contest, and we recognize and honor the final fifteen stories in this compilation with extreme gratitude. Please enjoy what you are about to read, and don't forget to look up!

The Lumberloft

Smote in Sapulpa

by Christian Ulstrup

The story that I'm about to tell you is true...every word. With some cursory Googling, you'll be able to find secondary accounts—strangely, the details are on linked pages beyond the first. This particular story, it seems, is an algorithmic edge case, one that's not search engine-optimized. This is perhaps because it is, at its core, something that happened that was truly strange, of which you may glimpse flashes at the end of YouTube's long tail.

There are clips, seconds-long ones filmed vertically, with views in the double digits and no descriptions—these are the best, though I won't spoil the challenge of finding them. Narrower slices still can be found in a moderately trafficked nook of Tumblr. There is a blog post with still images—blurry, compressed snapshots of the thing that happened on March 2, with a sentence fragment approximating "something-something art exhibit gone awry something-something" for context.

So. What happened exactly? What happened exactly is a challenge for me—for anyone who was there—to communicate to anyone who wasn't there at the scene. Though, I can provide some color and tell you what I saw, how I saw it (and, really, how I think I saw it). And the reason, as I think you'll soon agree, that the objective what-happened, the Truth-with-a-capital-T eludes me is because every data point that I collected with my eyes and ears was stuck to an anecdote or recollection, further back in time, and I had to descend to my proverbial hands and knees to dig that adjacent datum from the proverbial ground (interviewees' minds mostly, at least the ones who would speak to me). In that state of contorted genuflection, I could have just kept on forever, but then my editor (and most importantly, my fiancée, Kate) began bitching at me to finish the damned piece because I was getting a bit "opposite-of-resourceful" with my research and—said Kate—a bit obsessed. That my dinner conversation had become a bit trying.

So, then. Fine. Let's talk about what happened. Let's start at the end, which is also the beginning, at an open-air art gallery in Sapulpa, Oklahoma, on March 2 of last year...

Sapulpa is windswept, with a clear sky overhead and a chill through my blue plaid shirt. It's like this every year, from winter until later than my coastal peers would guess. There are sudden changes through the summers—phase shifts, as is said —that plant along the panhandle state's plain furious vortices, funnels unseen until they begin whipping up dirt and livestock and my cousin's distant neighbors' double-wides. Tornadoes leave behind destruction of biblical proportions (which, even as an unbelieving Californian, I say without sarcasm). These 'scapes demand a fear of God; there are whole neighborhoods, once-whole, made into flattened parcels of land and smithereens.

Flattened, yes...that's a good segue to the event—this thing that happened at the art gallery.

The gallery is en plein air, is brimming with white people, features outsider art,

and is sponsored by a local gypsum heiress. Her name is Merrill McCormick. She was described to me as "aloof," floating at a stature above her five feet and eleven inches, and, as my cousin alleged, "developed a taste for high-brow stuff" during a semester far away from Oral Roberts University, in Lyons (weekend trips to Paris piqued it, I think?). My sleight cousin, ambling through the American Southwest and his extended adolescence, has invited me with a lower-cased email to stay with him for a few days "to escape the smog of los angeles" (he's never been). He's an exhibitor.

When I sidestep into the gallery, he's away, perhaps in an outhouse; but on a dirty-tornado-colored stucco wall—his modest patch—is an eerie oil of rocks in Sedona at dusk. The rocks are dark purple instead of the usual carmine, and I think that he really might sell this piece for four figures. It's poignant. Except, of course, for the gaudy faux antlers stuck to the frame. I mean, really, Fred? I make a mental note. A couple beside me twangs soft words of approval. I take a step back to appreciate the grand scale of what he's made and wonder if the antlers are not fake. A gunshot, somewhere, cracks. (I drove a copper Murano from a Hertz at the Tulsa airport and noticed two traffic signs with bullet holes.) There is a thud.

Startled, I take another step, and my heel digs into something that is not the Earth. It is the bottom of a black leather cowboy boot, turned skyward. This is part of an effigy. It is facedown. The effigy is dressed in dark blue Levi's and a plaid shirt—Buffalo Plaid like a scarecrow's. There's a wedding ring on the wrong hairy-knuckled hand—what attention to detail. It's part of a larger scene—one I'd not caught from the corner of my eye when I'd walked in—elaborate and sort of hilarious, especially compared to what the other exhibitors present: plains of all shades of green and brown, austere Indian portraits, a peppering of fist-sized heads in clay.

This thing is multi-dimensional, but perfectly placed. Equidistant from everything is a scene straight outta Looney Tunes. There is, as I've said, a facedown male effigy, the top half of which—forehead to collar—is buried by a cartoonish anvil, all of these things at satirical angles. I snort.

"Gene?"

I'm squatting by the elaborate sculpture and, knees flared, look up at Fred. He is beside a pulchritudinous thirty-something—obviously Ms. (Mrs.?) McCormick. She knows how to be tall. Her outfit is a white tee, jeans, gray heather Allbirds, and a leather jacket. Her lips are apart.

Fred speaks at a clip. "Gene, this is Merrill. We've just arrived..."

The wrong-handed ring finger twitches, and Merrill's eyes widen.

I stand.

She is gasping, and then she is shrieking. Merrill's shrieks are sharp—and more startling than that gunshot—although, I get the strange sense that she's rather calling attention to herself than emoting. She glances at me for a split second, to see if I'm looking.

I turn back to the anvil and the effigy, which is not an effigy. It's a man, a real-life man whose head has been crushed—

—annihilated—by an anvil embossed with A-C-M-E.

Merrill takes Fred's hand, Fred takes my hand, and we beeline through

a

gathering storm of lookers-on. Behind us are gasps and staccato profanities.

"Fred," Merrill says, wiping her eyes. "Fred, we must—Gene, my dear, please bear with me." She clasps her hands.

"Your car," Fred says to me. "Now."

Fred's words are like an insidious undertow, and I'm in no rush to drown. I do as I'm told.

I am thoroughly confused, but without alternatives. So, at Fred's instruction, I drive to Merrill's.

She is crying in the back of my rental, and Fred murmurs directions out of the hatched roads of downtown Sapulpa until we land on a stretch of asphalt, black as night, between sparse McMansions that make for something that resembles a suburb.

"There." Fred points at a gated driveway.

Merrill exits the car and punches a code into a box by the gate.

"Fred, what—?"

"Wait." He turns toward me, past me, his pupils like pinholes. I'd never before noticed at our yearly Thanksgiving dinners in Pittsburgh that his eyes were such a violent shade of green. The gate swings open, she gets back in, and we wind up the first hill I've seen all day. Merrill is silent. There is no crying.

Once in the house, Merrill scurries up a flight of stairs. I pace the foyer, tiptoeing between the setting's constituent parts. It is a strange blend of modern art and African statuettes. My mind jumps to "race." Though I don't know what to make of it. There is a photo of a young couple that is Merrill and someone else—he is happy; he is shorter

than she.

"Fred? Fre-ed," I call, cupping my mouth.

Fred had gone upstairs, too, and motioned at me to stay put. There is a muffled volley behind a closed door on the second floor. Merril's voice crescendos into something accusatory, and then Fred monotones. This repeats.

I go in circles. The first floor is large and small, and I catalog the items in each room. I code them; there are themes. To the right of the foyer is a living room with patterned wallpaper—lilies with ropey vines intertwined against a matte mauve—and a bear. The bear is immense, lumbering, taxidermied. The fireplace is choked with ash. There is an olive chaise lounge beside a reading window. Next, in the kitchen, there is a granite-topped island. It has not been used in a long time. On the top of a Mr. Coffee is a thin film of dust. Above the stove, hanging, is a crucifix. It is uncomfortably large, and Jesus has six-pack abs. The last room in the circuit is a sunlit study with massive windows and three-foot stacks of manila envelopes, fat with loose leaves of paper. There is a map on the wall, stapled to corkboard, with red-headed pins stuck in American metropoli and yarn strung up in between.

I have returned to the foyer. I take another lap.

Fred is in the foyer. "The cops," he says. "Are coming."

"The cops?"

"Merrill called them."

"Why?"

"Let's go. Let's go to the guest house." He is lean; he flexes his jaw.

That evening, Fred and I sit on the porch of a guest house near the gated entrance where Merrill has set him up, going on three months. She has been returned from the police station and, I would assume, is in her home. It is clear to me, though never stated by Fred, that she and I are not to interface, although Fred is a trusted intercessor. A gatekeeper, more like.

The sky is darkly golden and shimmering, on the cusp of winking out.

"Did you see the bone fragments?" Fred asks.

"Bone fragments?"

"The bits of brain?" He sips at two neat jiggers of Bulleit Rye.

I don't remember anything so grotesque; in my recollection, the scene was a chuckle-worthy imitation of Ron Mueck. It was an unbelievable deconstruction. A farce, even. Some commentary on something of local importance.

"Fred."

"Yes?"

"Those antlers," I say. "I did not care for them."

"What antlers?"

In that moment, I question everything. "The frame, Fred."

"Oh, you mean my painting?"

I nod.

"I fished it from a dump."

I chew on that. "Are you making fun of them?"

"Who?"

"The locals. The other artists."

"It seemed apropos." His Ps pop.

"You've never been funny, Fred."

Fred places his whiskey tumbler on the arm of his rocking chair and leans toward the porch railing.

I am anxious. "Watch it now. It'll spill."

"I'm paying attention."

"Are you?"

He chews on that. "You're right," he says.

"About what?"

"The antlers."

I rock. "How'd you get to the gallery?"

Fred sits back in the chair and catches his glass as it slides down the arm. He finishes what's left. "We drove. In Merrill's car."

"What was that all about? Making me drive you two—"

"We were high, Gene. I was high, and Merrill was too." He flicks the glass with his forefinger. "There was crank in the car."

"I'm sorry?"

"Crank, speed, ice." His lips thin. "Meth, Jeannie. I told you, we were high."

I am not surprised, but not as disappointed as I should be, either.

"You know, I've been productive since I've been here. Two paintings a week, at least."

I think about the inside of the guest house, where there are undoubtedly more deliverables that I'd ever guess Fred would have been able to conjure, though most of them are unfinished—rather products of his trailing off at the denouement of a high than works-in-progress. There is also an assortment of raw materials: pencil boxes, blank canvases, an unformed hunk of clay, a stack of shrink-wrapped oil paint tubes. "Have you ever even tried to sculpt anything?"

"She'd rather I'm well-resourced than the opposite," Fred says.

My mind's eye becomes focused on Merrill. "Fred, what the hell are you up to?"

He lets out a sigh and exposits: Five years ago, Merrill had been married to a man named Vincent (Vince), but never took his last name. Vince apparently has been crushed by an anvil at his estranged wife's art show. Now, in between those two events, Vince had left Merrill. He'd been in the midst of a frenzied exit when Fred, en route from Albuquerque to the Mark Twain National Forest, had met Merrill at a restaurant called Nonesuch, where they were dining by themselves. Merrill was distraught, and Fred was flirting with homelessness. (Fred has always had a nose for rich people who cannot handle their wealth.)

Fred says that Merrill "may be aloof," but is in fact afflicted by some sort of disorder wherein abandonment causes her unbearable psychic pain. And so really, by inviting himself to live with her under the guise of patronage, he was "doing her good," or some such sequence of mental gymnastics. To his credit, he seems to have stuck the landing. Regardless, he'd come to live with her, and they'd grown close. Some evenings, the two of them quite intoxicated, Merrill would oscillate between wailing at Fred to help her get Vince back (he was unreachable) and asking Fred to help her murder him—and if she could not, then God surely would. "God will smite him for what he's done, the Sodomite." Fred has always seemed to me obviously gay, so I took this to mean that his host was without irony—a monster. They made some half-baked plans—"A joke, a joke," Fred says—but then they were coming down, and they never finished the conversations. And then Vince's skull was crushed, and here we are.

What my cousin has said to me has a bizarre sort of logic to it. I can find no obvious lie, and I take each statement at face value; though they sum to something uncanny, like a Jenga tower in a game that has gone on far too long, where the stack of blocks appears an affront to cosmic law, but—for some stomach-churning reason—will not topple.

We each have one more glass, grumble trivia, and reminisce about family gatherings in Pittsburgh. Then suddenly it's the next morning, and I am in seat 11C on the plane back to LAX. I glance out at the tarmac and text my editor: "New scoop. Need a few weeks for research. Where am I re travel budget. About to take off hold on"

He responds, "No travel bdgt at moment. Ok. Call when u land"

Three weeks later, I am in my home office, lost in a deluge of sticky notes, fragmented interview transcripts, photographs, email threads, and a smattering of other digitized data that are burying the lede of my article. I am going in circles.

I conduct phone interviews, peruse comments below Sapulpa Times articles.

Things grow stranger. (I bring them up at dinner. Kate is vexed.)

There is a Sapulpa trebuchet society: It is called the Sapulpan Assembly (of

Trebuchet Enthusiasts). They launch heavy objects. They say they aim those things away from Sapulpa, away from Sapulpans. I take two phone calls with the organizers. They are forty-minute phone calls. I do not know what is a joke and what is not. They seem serious; their accents are endearing, disarming.

Merrill is a minority stakeholder in hundreds of companies, including one that ships and insures expensive trinkets via a fleet of retired Cessnas. There is another one that manufactures movie props. In Tennessee, there is an arthouse movie in production. It is a live-action take on Wile E. Coyote and the Road Runner—a commentary on gender (what?). This is interesting. It is also circumstantial, and I cannot make inroads with the companies, project owners, or showrunners. I doubt my ability. The world between the coasts is impenetrable.

Locals are talkative until they're not. I reach out to a few, and then their neighbors, family members, and colleagues start reaching out to me. They want to set the record straight: Merrill is good; her husband had succumbed to the Devil's temptations. Vince was a known homosexual, even before he married Merrill. Also, denial is a river in Africa. Merrill is rumored to have a new beau. And she won't return my calls. Fred has moved out of her guest house (and toward Brooklyn) and falls out of range of my emails; this is not unusual.

All but one of my follow-up emails go unanswered. A man calls me from a blocked number, tells me that Vince had been drunk with him at a covert gay bar. He had confided in him his suicidal ideation. He was ashamed and asked the man, a civil engineer, if it were technically feasible to construct a guillotine with materials from Home Depot. He invited the man to a Motel 6. The caller had declined. This was two weeks before the outsider art show.

I get ahold of the local sheriff.

"Sheriff Culkin speaking."

"Hello, Sheriff Culkin," I say. "This is Gene Palumbo. I'm a reporter."

He pauses. "What can I do for ya?"

"I'm calling about Vince—"

"Oh," he says. "I know who you are."

Word has gotten around.

"Look," he says.

"Yes?"

"That whole...that was unfortunate, what happened to Vince. But I don't think you'll find what you're looking for."

"And what's that?"

"We don't talk to reporters, see."

"You're talking to one now."

"Mr. Palumbo," the sheriff twangs. "God's got a strange way of willing things. And I hope you can respect that. Us. Our community, I mean. I wish you the best, I really do." Click.

I am anxious to wrap my research, to publish something. I wait for weeks for someone else to broadcast the story, but no one does. There is a short article in the Sapulpa Times about the art exhibit, with as many words dedicated to critiquing (praising) the art as accounting for Merrill's estranged husband's bizarre demise. "An unfortunate accident," the author concluded.

I wake up to three missed calls from one of the trebuchet society organizers. I call him back but only get his voicemail. The same thing happens the following night. I send text messages. I receive none back, and that's the last I hear from him. According to an IMDB thread, the movie has gone into production hell. The Times article is no longer available; it has been "archived." I think about the antlers on my cousin's frame.

Is this a conspiracy? Between who? About what?

Did drugs play a role? Well, of course, but maybe only a supporting role. Every detail is a red herring. Or not.

Finally, I am out of time, out of funds. I have these facts:

Vince is dead, crushed by an anvil.

A coroner ruled the death an accident.

Merrill is unreachable. Fred is unreachable.

It is September.

Now, the truth is, when I sent first, second, and third drafts of this story to my editor, he feigned constructive feedback...each time, about as nonplussed. Although, it wasn't until the fourth round that I realized that he'd never publish my story.

"G., where's the third act?" he said in an email. So I did a page one rewrite in a flash. I dropped the journalistic terseness and sketched it how I saw it. Then I happened upon LumberLoft. And here we are: you, reading this piece, having expected boutique lit. And me, most likely still trying to figure out what in God's name actually happened at, around, before, and—perhaps most puzzlingly—above that outsider art show in Sapulpa.

I mentioned I'm not a believer, but what I experienced in March—what informed this written estimation—was so utterly bizarre that it has put me in a bit of a mood. I am struck with something existential. I am unsettled. But I figure that maybe someone out there can put a little more structure around the details of the event, dig data from the Oklahoman plain, and stack 'em with a tenuous grip until they make for an incontrovertible answer. Was this an act of man, an act of God, or an Act of God?

Anyway, if you really are interested in pursuing this thing, drop me a note. You won't find my contact details here, but they are out there—if you're serious, you'll figure out where to look. And don't spook the locals. Godspeed.

A Trail

by Rocco Blue

Sam still owned a flip phone, and she didn't know how to turn off silent mode. So, every time her boss sent her a text message, she giggled because the phone's vibrate setting tickled her leg through her pocket. This usually happened while she was riding her bike and usually in the middle of an assignment. During one giggle while at the red light of 42nd Avenue and 54th Street, Mrs. Hayfield saw the laughing fit from her porch, and to her, the giggling was spontaneous and not provoked by an old cell phone.

Mrs. Hayfield, who had always been a bit paranoid, became convinced that Sam was laughing at her orange-and-blue muumuu. Sam rode on, thinking nothing of her own seemingly spontaneous laugh, not even aware of Mrs. Hayfield's presence. Mrs. Hayfield sat on her porch for another forty minutes and thought about the laugh while zero cars passed by on the normally busy street. She went inside, trapped her sixteen cats in the corner of the garage, and ate each one alive—including the bones and fur—while each cat watched in a frenzy of hisses and moans as the old lady devoured its brothers and sisters like a possessed demon.

Legitimate jobs had become ridiculously hard to find since Sam's DUI, so she had taken to illegal dealings that paid cash and involved unmarked boxes and weird-smelling envelopes. It was creepy stuff, in her opinion, but she didn't ask questions. She was just happy that she could make money by riding her bike every day, and the huffing of tennis ball gas definitely helped her get on with her work in a way that was lucid and not at all stiff or tense. She hated being tense.

Sam didn't have much of a political stance. If she did have one, she guessed she would've named her personal political party The Severed Rubber Bands. Her party's motto would've been: That's right, motherfuckers, we're anti-tension.

Without GPS on the ancient phone, she printed Google directions from her house and carried them in her pocket on the ride. Today's delivery was a far ride. It was two hours west through a part of the county she was not familiar with.

She washed the oil off her hands with orange soap and pressed the garage door button. The mechanical whir of the lifting door scared her cat, and it scurried outside into the cool November air. Sam cracked open two tennis ball canisters and huffed. The growing block of sunlight passed over her work bench and illuminated the white paint of her Flackondale Synapse, a bike coveted by all couriers, a bike she received as payment after her first job with Ms. Gomey.

Drool spontaneously erupted from the corner of her mouth in the form of a tiny geyser, and her spit landed on the nubs of her severed middle and ring finger. The fingers had been payment to Ms. Gomey after a failed merchandise transport two years earlier.

Sam considered wiping the drool on her pants, but decided to instead let it air dry.

She passed the airport and rode under the Robber Baron's Expressway. She rolled up to 42nd Avenue and 54th Street. Mrs. Hayfield was sitting on her porch covered in dried blood that was flaking off in large potato chip chunks. She smiled at Sam's profile and waved. Sam didn't notice. Her phone buzzed, and she scream-laughed. The light turned green. As Sam rode on toward the part of town with which she was unfamiliar, Mrs. Hayfield—still grinning inside in the blood shell—stood up and went inside her house. Mrs. Hayfield then ate all of her furniture. All of it: her couch, her bed, her kitchen table and its chairs, and her coffee table.

Sam passed 68th Street and officially entered unfamiliar territory. This was a weird move for Ms. Gomey. Sam was pretty sure that the Serling Family operated in this part of town.

The bike lane was unsure of itself, pounding along unabated for a couple of miles, then petering off into nothingness, and then reappearing. She groaned at the asphalt, knowing just where this was going, and it was disconcerting.

This part of town hadn't had any roadwork for years. Sam could tell not only by the fading road lines, ill-designed bike lanes, and traffic lights straight out of 1970s era Mister Rogers' Neighborhood. She could tell that this part of town hadn't had any roadwork for years because there were zero cars and there were gaping pot holes, some as big as swimming pools, with screeching purple creatures that had long arms with sharp claws, each dragging a sack-like legless torso behind it out of the holes.

"The whole area is going to be wonky," she said to herself.

Sam was grateful for the weather though. The Florida sun beat down onto her,

but a cool breeze took the edge off. She couldn't remember what street she was taking

the right on. At the red light, she pulled the directions out of her pocket.

RIGHT ON FELDER LANE.

The light turned green, and Sam rode on. She passed by a lone boombox sitting on the edge of the road that was blasting out "The Rhythm of the Night" by Corona.

"Why that song?" she asked herself as the wind rushed through her hair.

The city left her riddled with anxiety, but the suburbs made her even edgier. She hated the rows of low-rise buildings designed to resemble old-town main streets.

Why the hell did they have fake upper-level windows, as if the operators of the chain restaurants went upstairs after work, cooked themselves a soulful meal, and went to bed? It was like city planners and architects were existentially frightened and wanted so desperately to hide the nightmares and alienation of society that their creations came off as overcompensations of trying to hide the nightmares and alienation.

Sam stopped in front of the Burger Wankers with fake upper-level windows, picked up a rock, and threw it at the center window. The window shattered, and the glass exploded into the apartment above the Burger Wankers and out of the apartment, the shards of window trickling through the rod iron of the fake balcony rail. An old man with a big gut covered by a white tank top popped his head outside the broken window and screamed at her while shaking his fist.

Sam grimaced, yanked on her collar, gulped, and quickly jumped back onto her bike.

Days like this made her feel like she would never escape the American game

and that she would spend the remainder of her days on a bike while slowly losing her appendages.

Sam turned right onto Felder Lane and passed an ancient gas station that looked like it had been transplanted there from a fake neighborhood in a nuclear test site from the 1950s. At night, Sam bet, this facility would shudder to life. Purple and orange lights would audibly crunch to their "on" positions.

A buzz-saw screech would shake the foundation and reverberate into the neighborhood, shaking the houses. People in hard hats would tumble from the building, flicking their noses at each other like secretive Santas. The shadows of the intricate tube system wrapped the building's steel staircases, and the cinderblock façade crossed each other. The shadows made X's on each crew member's face.

The man waving the lit torches reminded her of a remote airport in the center of Antarctica.

A little boy was crying on the curb, his head on his knees. Sam stopped.

"Are you okay?" she asked him. The boy looked up from his knees and wiped snot away with his shirt sleeve.

"No," he said. "I can't find my house."

"Do you know your address?" Sam asked. She pulled out her phone and checked the time. It was 11:42 a.m. The package had to be delivered no later than 12:45 p.m., and she was pretty sure she hadn't even reached the halfway point yet.

"Yeah," the boy said and pointed at the southwestern ranch-style house behind him. "It's here." Sam surveyed the road. Dead end. She pulled out the directions.

"Are you screwing around, kid?" Sam asked while scanning the paper. "I don't have time for this."

"This is my address, but this is not my house," he said. Sam folded the paper and stuffed it back into her pocket.

"You're really funny," she told him and gave a reassuring smile. "The economy will pick up, and you guys will be on your feet again."

The boy looked at his feet and then rested his head back onto his knees. Across the lawn, the house appeared to have a couple of adults standing in the window watching them. She looked down the road at the yellow barricade.

"Do you know how to get onto Greenway Bike Trail?" she asked the boy. "My directions say it's just at the end of Felder."

"It is," the boy said into his knees.

"But there's a barricade."

"You have to go around the barricade," the boy said. "What happened to your fingers?"

Sam pushed her bike onward, ignoring his question. "Thanks. Hope you find your house."

Sam stopped at the dead end and stepped off her bike. She walked around the barricade into the patchy grass, crunching on the leaves and acorns. There was no path, just trees. She walked her Flackondale into the forest and looked up at the swaying branches. The sun was shielded by gray clouds, and late November revealed itself as the breeze rolled in. Sam shivered and turned. The neighborhood and the little boy disappeared behind the trees. She pressed on. The even clicking of her bike's gear cluster offset the imbalance of nature's clamor.

Sam pushed through the limbs of the two hugging shrubs and stepped out of the woods onto a trail. She pulled the moss and grime from the trail sign.

GREENWAY BIKE TRAIL.

There were no markings, and there was no map. She was a little creeped out by this, but figured the trail was an old one. She hopped onto her bike and pedaled on. The trail was surrounded by more forest and ran along a river she was unfamiliar with. It wasn't the Hillsgrove River, and she was sure that there weren't any other rivers in the county.

There weren't any houses set into the forest. Sam wasn't very familiar with the area, but she was almost certain that there were no large parks or undeveloped sections over here. This whole district had been staked out and built up over twenty years ago by Stale Incorporated.

The vast desolation of untouched land stretched out ahead of her, ambling along the bumpy dirt path.

Most of her job's packages were lightweight, and she never noticed them in her backpack, but today's package was heavy. As time passed, it felt like it was growing heavier. She rounded a corner, and in the distance the forest opened to a field with a large factory sitting in the middle. Smoke plumed from the twin stacks, and cranking sounds of industry echoed from the building across the field.

The river exploded. The water, the scum, and the rest of its contents fired out of

the hollowed-out line of Earth. The river gushed and rolled into a wave through the woods. It followed closely behind Sam, chasing her. The Flackondale's tires popped, and she wobbled, skidding across the dead leaves. She rolled slowly to a cumbersome crank and then to a spinning of her pedals that moved the mud under the back tire instead of moving her.

"No." The wave hit her, knocking her and her bike down. They slid through the forest, scraping over rocks and tree roots. The water coiled around her and crashed over her from all sides. Sam jumped up out of the water. She coughed and spit up murky water. She hoisted her heavy backpack up her back, tightened the straps, and picked up her bike. The river crashed over her again. She braced herself on the bike and let the water wash over her as she held her breath.

Cloaked people rose from the mud next to her. They stepped forward. The mud dripped from their boots as they crept toward her. She ran with the bike at her side, cranking along over the wet, uneven terrain. The water flowed over her, rushing ahead, rising over her ankles, up her legs. The entire forest seemed to be flooded.

The package had grown as it hung in a lump, sagging in the bottom of her pack. The cool November air stung her wet skin, and the shade of the trees made it worse the deeper in she ran. Hands rose from the water and reached for her as she sloshed across the woods. Hands emerged from the trees, passing through the trunks, through the bark.

A house revealed itself to her in the distance as the water became more violent, crashing into her sides, trying to knock her over. She jumped over the hands and leapt in between the wraiths as they separated from the trees and turned toward her. The echoing of synchronized exhalation crashed over her.

It was an angry, yet calm breathing that rose in volume and pounded into her ears.

The breath finally dissipated into a noisy mist as the front door opened, and the boy stepped out into the forest. He waved Sam inside.

"Hurry," he yelled at Sam. The water crashed into Sam's side and knocked her over her bike. The chain popped loose. Sam kicked one of the hands reaching up for her and jumped into the boy's arms. She rolled the bike through the front door and let it loose, hearing some glass shatter as it hit something in the living room. The boy pulled Sam inside and shut the door. Sam fell to the flooded living room floor and splashed in the water.

"What's happening?" Sam yelled and took the boy's hand. "Are you seeing that? Am I crazy?" The boy hoisted her up, and as he did so, he grew taller into a teenage boy. He sneezed in Sam's face. His clothes had grown with him from blue shorts and a Teenage Mutant Ninja Turtles shirt to a red polo and blue jeans.

"Sorry," the boy said. "Ms. Gomey sent you."

Sam wiped the snot away. "It's fine."

The house was succumbing to rapid decay, just shy of instantaneous. Mold moved across the furniture and fired up the wall. Even the teenage boy was set into the advances of old growth. He grew before her eyes into a man...and then an old man. Fibers fell from his suit. His hair twisted and crusted into matted chunks. His skin fell into itself, settling into deep wrinkles before Sam's eyes.

The weight of the backpack pulled Sam down well past the point of comfort. Sam set it down and knelt beside it. She unzipped the pack and reached in. The old man coughed and sat down in the chair next to her.

"I think this place is dying," he said.

Sam struggled to pull the box out of the pack. Its weight was greater than at least a hundred pounds, but the box was only as large as the palm of her hand.

"Go to sleep, my baby," Sam said while staring at the package.

"I don't remember," the old man said, his voice now cracked and dry. "I miss my mommy." Sam looked up at him, and the old man sunk into the chair. His skin collapsed into his bones. A floundered breath escaped him, and the man crumbled away into dust.

Sam scrambled and tore open the box. Dust puffed out of it. She reached in and felt around. There was only dust. The house decayed, and the old growth of the forest overtook, returning the materials to nature.

The cloaked people emerged from the trees. Two speckled green birds crossed the path from the east, and one green bird followed, crossing the path from the west.

Sam jumped back and felt around in the tall grass for her bike. The chirping echoed into the dank wilderness of muted green. Moss hanging from the oaks swung in the wind. Deconstructed quilts of brown leaves billowed and rose, tucking her feet into the habitat.

She felt the chain and pulled it off the gear cluster. The river crashed over her and flung her into a tree. The cloaked figures all at once ran toward her. She whipped the first one with her chain and slashed open its robe. Dust poured from the open wound and fell in a wet clump to the Earth.

The wraiths continued forward, reaching for her. She screamed and jumped, grabbing a low-hanging tree branch. She swung and kicked two of the cloaked men, knocking them back only a couple feet. She leapt to the next branch.

The hands came forth through the bark of the tree and grabbed her body.

She forgot about her cats. She forgot about Ms. Gomey. She forgot about her love and her hope. There was nothing else. The faintest spark of a memory of her own hands holding a forgotten object grew and then died. The hands pulled harder.

She felt her bones shattering, and she fantasized about dying. She let out one last breath as her organs mashed.

The birds chirped loudly in her ears.

Sam felt the sharp squeeze of all pain, and she saw the green and brown growth of the world. The void overtook her, and the hands pulled her all the way in.

She saw herself from above: Viscera, blood, and crushed bones poured from the breaks in her compounded skin. The hands pulled and pounded, pulverizing what was once Sam into a pink compost.

The river water rushed up the tree, washing her remains away. The water gushed through the woods, across the bike trail, and deposited back into the river basin.

The foamy mess of her separated parts swirled into itself, and she rematerialized. It was an ill-formed goopy version of herself. Her missing middle and ring fingers grew out of the nubs. Her body solidified, and she smiled.

Thought Bubbles

by Sue Mitchell

The grey-black iridescent beads piled up in a corner of the shower stall. Mary first thought they were soap suds, but they didn't dissolve. She poked at them with her toe before picking them up for a closer inspection. Shortsightedly holding them close, she peered at them. Colours swirled inside, slowly revolving, alive and sentient. Startled, Mary dropped them into the sink where they dulled. She gingerly rinsed them in tepid water. Intrigued, she left them in a saucer and prepared for work.

#

In the car, she noticed more of the beads. The size of marbles, the colours within writhed. Mary collected them into a pile on the passenger seat. Was it her imagination, or did they huddle together?

Mary focused on her driving. She hated driving, or more accurately, she hated other drivers. She considered them all incompetent, while her driving skills were masterful. When she parked and glanced at the beads, they seemed to have increased in number, but that was impossible. She scooped them into a discarded grocery bag. They were warm to the touch and almost humming. No sound, but a vibration. Maybe. She tucked the bag out of sight in the footwell. At least they couldn't roll away; the bag kept them secure.

#

Riding the elevator to the seventeenth floor gave Mary the opportunity to appraise her coworkers. None of them were, in her opinion, fit to do the job. Lazy, incompetent, careless, and useless. Had she been in charge, she would have fired them all. She had nothing but contempt for any of them, either above or below her in the company hierarchy.

Stepping out of the elevator, she trod on a bead, which silently exploded, releasing a stench like a well-ripened fart. Those remaining cast looks of disgust, but the doors closed before she could explain.

A few beads scattered on the floor by her feet. As she knelt to scoop them up, they rolled towards her, like ducklings towards a mother duck. She deposited them gently into her suit jacket pocket.

Mary's workspace was an anonymous cubicle; she didn't merit her own office. If status was accorded to quality and quantity of work, she deserved a corner suite with river views. The imbecile currently inhabiting that space was utterly useless. Mary knew that her boss only held his position because he had a half-competent personal assistant. In Mary's opinion, the P.A. wasn't worth her salary either, but she looked the part. Mary mused that creating the right impression was infinitely more important these days than skills or talent.

Her computer went through its interminable setting-up processes while Mary carefully hung her suit jacket on a padded hanger that hooked over the cubicle wall. Her supervisor bustled towards her. Mary ducked down, but maybe the supervisor wasn't heading to her specifically. The bloody woman was always complaining about something. Mary would love to tell her what she really thought, but a single woman with a mortgage had to hold her opinions to herself if she wanted to keep her job.

"Mary! Did you step in dog poop on your way in? There's a nasty trail from the lift to here. Call maintenance to send a cleaning crew. God, how can you stand it?" Carol, Mary's supervisor teetered away on her four-inch heels, holding a hand over her nose.

Automatically, Mary lifted her shoes to check. She couldn't see or smell anything, but she noticed her colleagues stifling smirks. She ran an unmanicured finger down the laminated list of extension numbers and called maintenance. Slamming down the phone, she saw another bead roll lazily across her desk. Colours within writhed and glowed darkly. Mary felt a vibration in her skull. She deftly collected the bead and placed it with the others in her jacket pocket.

The cleaning crew came and went; sullen, rude, and inefficient. Mary thought their liberal application of air freshener was both unnecessary and impertinent. She fired off an email to the head of maintenance to complain rather than to thank them for a speedy response.

By lunchtime, Mary had accrued a handful more of the mysterious glowing beads. She slipped them into her pocket as she prepared to leave. Depending on the weather, she usually ate her lunch either sitting in her car or on a park bench. Today she went directly to her car to add the clutch of beads to the others. The weather was glorious—sunny with a light breeze, too pleasant to huddle in her car. She headed for her usual bench, and as always, she spread a cloth before sitting.

Bloody pigeons crap everywhere. Vermin. That's what they are, bloody vermin. Someone should poison them all! Well, hello. Where did you come from? Yet another iridescent bead rolled next to Mary, oily colours roiling within. She picked it up and held it between her thumb and forefinger. You really are beautiful, aren't you? The bead pulsed, and Mary felt the vibration deep in her core. Bloody pigeons! The bead pulsed vigorously in response. A bird fell out of the tree, stone dead, startling the others into flight. The bead faded to an inky blackness and stopped pulsating. Dead. Mary frowned as an intriguing thought swam from the murky depths of her mind.

As the pigeons resettled on the nearby branches, Mary closed her eyes and allowed herself—encouraged herself—to think about them. She imagined them spreading filth and disease in their wake, how she wished a civic-minded individual would poison them. Opening her eyes, she saw a fresh scattering of beads. No, not beads. Thought bubbles. These were her thoughts manifested. She concentrated on imagining all the pigeons dying, flicking her eyes between the birds fluttering to the ground, and the thought bubbles dimming in corresponding numbers confirmed her theory. Bloody Hell!

Mary jumped to her feet, scattering the dead thought bubbles, and turned to look at her office building. What if it works on more than pigeons? Will it work on people? Do I have that power?

Mary intended to punish them all, but her first experiment would be Carol. Carol and her four-inch bloody heels. Carol and her effortlessly sleek blond bob. Carol and her shapely legs and trim waist. Carol and her superiority complex that masked her inadequacy. She really shouldn't have humiliated me this morning. I'll make her pay for that.

Mary barged her way into an already crowded elevator car, eager to reach the seventeenth floor and test her exciting new theory. She'd bring Carol down a peg or two. Nothing permanent...just a little humiliation, something to dent her pride.

Mary heard the commotion as soon as the elevator doors slid open. A woman was crying, and voices, both male and female, were raised in consternation. A group had gathered around Carol, who lay on the floor whimpering.

"Just hold on, sweetheart. Help is on its way, it won't be long. There, there. You'll be alright."

The P.A. from the corner office had taken charge. She shepherded two of the managers in front of her, instructing them to lift Carol and carry her to the nearest conference room, where they placed her in a comfortably padded chair. Mary moved to her desk, disappointed to have missed the show, but thrilled that her experiment had worked. Carol slipping and spraining an ankle could be a coincidence, but Mary didn't think so. She hugged herself tightly and smiled, before remembering to assume a somber expression. Looking gleeful about Carol's downfall wouldn't be politic.

When she rehung her suit jacket, she found a dead thought bubble in the pocket. It hadn't been there while she ate her lunch, of that she was certain. Once the paramedics had carted Carol away, the afternoon passed slowly. The initial buzz of excitement faded quickly, leaving a void that idle gossip couldn't adequately fill.

Mary efficiently emptied her in-tray and worked uninterrupted on her proposal to streamline the department. With Carol away, Mary saw an opportunity to step up the ladder, to demonstrate her efficiency and clarity of vision.

#

Shrewdly virtuous, Mary packed tomorrow's lunch. Taking a packed lunch had multiple benefits: you didn't pay inflated prices for substandard meals; you used up leftovers again, saving money; but most importantly, you chose where to eat. Mary had eaten in the cafeteria but had always been uncomfortable. Conversations stuttered when she approached, people no doubt intimidated by her innate superiority. She was more comfortable eating alone, but that didn't mean she didn't feel the sting of being an outcast. Yeah, the cafeteria crowd. Mary wanted them to experience some of the discomfort they'd inflicted upon her. Mary's eyes widened with pleasure and surprise when a pulsating thought bubble rolled across the kitchen counter to rest next to her lunchbox.

#

Mary took longer than usual in the shower, applying conditioner to her hair and shaving her legs, things she usually skipped as unnecessary. She planned to use all possible weapons in her arsenal to impress while Carol was out of commission. If stupid fripperies such as a hair conditioner and lipstick would help win over her idiot bosses, she would use them. By the time she finished, the shower stall was overflowing with vibrating thought bubbles, humming like a nest of exotic insects. Mary carefully gathered each one and placed them in a pile on the countertop. The humming and swirling was hypnotic, and only with a great effort did Mary pull herself away.

When she made her bed, she found it infested with thought bubbles. When she held out her hand, they rolled towards her. A few stubbornly still dead ones turned to odourless ash when she tried to remove them. Before setting out for work, she checked the welfare of the lunchbox thought bubble, which was roiling and pulsating vigorously.

#

No one complimented her more polished appearance, but she caught a few nudges and smirks from the corner of her eye. Mary ignored them. She cleared her in-tray in record time and spent the rest of the morning finessing her proposals. The document was a work of art with colourful charts and graphs to illustrate her ideas.

She watched the first lunch break crew with carefully controlled glee. Upon their return, she took her break, choosing to sit again on the pigeon popular bench. There were significantly fewer birds today. Impatient to get back and see the effect of her thought bubble, she returned early to her desk. A sour stench permeated the office, and many desks were empty with phones left to ring unanswered. Unprecedented. The bossy P.A. was not at her post. She was an early luncher. Mary watched with wide-eyed innocence as more personnel left their workstations unattended, some fleeing to different floors, when it became clear all the toilets on this floor were occupied—and would be for the foreseeable future.

She watched the lunchbox thought bubble slowly extinguish. Then she called emergency services, reporting a severe case of food poisoning. When the medics arrived, Mary made herself useful to them. It was early evening before anyone not hospitalised was fit enough to travel home. Mary had very much enjoyed herself, being an angel of mercy to her suffering colleagues.

When she eventually packed to leave, the thought bubble had disintegrated to a fine ash, which she easily blew away.

#

Mary celebrated her success with canned salmon and ice cream. She rarely indulged in desserts, but reasoned she deserved a treat, and tomorrow was shaping up to be a big day.

#

As Mary anticipated, few staff turned up for work. She went straight to the directors and informed them she would hire a few dozen temps for the next week or so, to at least keep things ticking over. Relieved someone was taking charge, they gave her carte blanche to do as she saw fit. She may not have been popular, but everyone knew she was efficient and company-oriented. For the next week, Mary was in heaven. The temps deferred to her, and the bosses were grateful. This is how her life ought to be. Finally, after years of service, she was being recognized and appreciated.

Then Carol came back. On crutches! Fearless and determined, Carol to the rescue. A woman on crutches. Everyone—directors and temps—thought she was a saint. You can't expect someone on crutches to do anything, so everyone fluttered around her, making sure she was comfortable and constantly caffeinated. Carol had the temerity to appropriate Mary's best temp as her own P.A. Speechless with barely suppressed fury, Mary sat in her cubicle amongst a rapidly growing collection of threateningly iridescent thought bubbles. They swarmed around her ankles and across her keyboard, increasingly animated. Now that Carol was back, Mary was invisible again.

#

Each night, the thought bubbles swarmed in Mary's bed, warming her. The lullaby of their chitinous quivering sent her to sleep, but she awoke tired each morning. Everyone noticed how she appeared aged in the last weeks. They attributed the premature ageing to stress. Carol, the directors, and the temps all gossiped and agreed that Mary wasn't coping with the extra responsibilities. Her work was still exemplary, but physically, Mary was deteriorating. Her skin was fragile and papery, her hair brittle and streaked with grey. She lost weight too. Never voluptuous, she was now skeletal. Blue veins showed on the backs of her hands. Mary saw the changes in herself, and they fuelled her fury. All she had sacrificed for the company, and still they refused to recognise her value.

#

Mary considered herself a fair and generous person and a good neighbour. She didn't speak to her neighbours, that's how good she was, no bother at all. The man who lived next door wasn't such a great neighbour. He had his television on full volume while he cheered for his football team. She heard several voices; he must have friends over. Inconsiderate bastards!

Mary stomped around to her neighbour's and battered on the door. Her beer-soused neighbour leaned on the jamb for support.

"I'm from next door. You're making my life impossible. I want you to turn down the sound on your television. And stop screaming and shouting. You do know the players can't hear you?" Mary leaned forward and stared him right in the eyes, daring him to defy her.

"Next door?" The swaying man squinted to bring Mary into focus. "Right! You must be Mary's mum! Come on in, join us, have a beer. Bring Mary—we've plenty of beer."

Humiliated and speechless, Mary turned to flee. Thought bubbles spilled incontinently from her pockets.

"Hey, lady! You're losing your marbles!" Giggling helplessly at his own humour, the neighbour staggered back to his guests.

Tears of frustration and humiliation cascaded down Mary's withered cheeks. To have her complaint ignored as though it was of no consequence! But to be mistaken for her own mother! Physical vanity was not one of Mary's vices, but this rapid ageing was horrifying.

Back in the security of her own kitchen, she could hear the whoops and cheers continuing from next door and convinced herself the laughter was at her expense. How dare they ignore her request, and how dare they laugh at her? She should have stayed and insisted he turn down the volume. Mary seethed and fumed at her impotence. Both colleagues and neighbours ignored her. There must be something she could do to teach him a lesson. All she'd asked him to do was to turn down the damned television.

Running the thought bubbles through her gnarled fingers, she took comfort from their hum and swirling colours. Their agitation increased with hers; they drew her in, mesmerising her.

A crash from next door broke the spell. Mary cocked her head, listening intently. No television, just male voices arguing. Mary smiled to herself. Quiet at last. The thought bubbles ceased to agitate and faded. She left them on the countertop to disintegrate with dignity. The hesitant knock on the door startled her. This was the first time anyone had knocked on her door. She considered ignoring it, but curiosity won out. The neighbour and his football fan friends had arrayed themselves outside her door, bearing cartons of beer and plundered pizza boxes.

"Missus, we wondered if we could move the party here. It's the final, and the telly just fell off the wall. Please?"

Several of the friends mutely offered the beer and pizza.

"Your television fell off the wall? That was the crash I heard?"

"Yes, ma'am."

Mary laughed out loud, throwing back her head and roaring her delight.

"Ma'am?"

"Fuck off!" Mary slammed the door on their astonished faces. Damn! That felt good.

Back in the kitchen, Mary swept the thought bubble dust into the sink and watched it swirl down the drain. Peace and quiet, with recognition of her power re-established.

As Mary lay in her bed, thought bubbles multiplied around her, their susurrations lulling her to sleep. She dreamed of bringing low her supercilious colleagues, of standing above them, alone and victorious.

She awoke weary, emaciated, and colourless. Swollen joints made moving slow and painful. Peering bleary-eyed into the bathroom mirror, Mary's physical deterioration startled her. A chill of horror replaced the euphoria from the previous evening.

#

Mary's appearance shocked Carol. She came straight over to Mary's cubicle and crouched next to her, pushing the crutches to one side. Mary was panting with the exertion of getting from her car to the lift, then from the lift to her workstation. She knitted together her fingers to stop their trembling.

"Oh, Mary, you really shouldn't be here. You should be at home...or in a hospital."

Mary wordlessly shook her head. Carol just wants to get rid of me. She doesn't really care about my well-being; it's just an act. She wants everyone to see how selfless she is, coming to work on crutches, being a martyr.

"Don't argue, Mary. It's decided. We'll get you home, call a doctor, and you can concentrate on getting well again. Rest, that's what you need, poor thing. Just give me a few minutes to get everything arranged, okay?"

Mary sat at her computer, too exhausted to switch it on. She closed her eyes and leaned back to await Carol's return. Mary determined to turn this to her advantage, to bring down Carol and the idiot bosses.

Carol turned up with one of the maintenance crew in tow. She put out her hand.

"I need your car keys. You're not fit to drive. Goodness only knows how you got here. Anyway, I'll drive you home, and Jimmy here will follow in your car. That way, you won't feel trapped." Carol smiled brightly. "Okay? Keys, please."

Mary nodded towards her handbag.

"In there. Keys are in there. Thank you. It's very good of you to take care of me like this."

Jimmy and Carol helped Mary to the lift and then to Carol's car, where they strapped her in for the silent ride home.

"Lucky I drive an automatic. I'd be buggered in a manual, what with this ankle."

Mary looked sideways at Carol, but otherwise didn't respond.

Jimmy carefully parked Mary's car, then helped Carol get her into the house. Carol noticed it was immaculate, except for random piles of fine, charcoal-coloured powder on saucers and plates. Was Mary doing drugs? Did that explain her unusual decline? Concerned for Mary's welfare, Carol snuck a peek in the fridge, thankful to see it was well-stocked. She shooed Jimmy outside to wait while she made Mary as comfortable as possible.

Carol herded Mary into the bedroom with instructions to get into bed. Minutes later, she came in with a tray. She'd made a plate of sandwiches and a thermos of coffee. She put Mary's phone next to the thermos.

"You've been neglecting yourself, Mary. Make sure you eat something. And call the doctor. Or would you like me to call now? It's no trouble."

Mary moaned and shook her head. Carol's ministrations irritated her. Who the hell does she think she is, taking charge like this, pretending to care so she'll look good to the bosses. Bitch. Mary fluttered a hand in dismissal.

"I'll call you tomorrow, Friday, to see how you're doing, okay? You've worked yourself into the ground, Mary, but you must rest now, put yourself first, okay? Right, well, I'll call tomorrow. Just call me if there's anything you need, okay?"

Mary closed her eyes while Carol backed awkwardly out of the room. Mary listened for the snick of the front door closing and the purr of Carol's car driving away.

"Jimmy, did you notice anything strange in Mary's home?"

"Strange? No, I don't think so...unless you mean it was freakishly tidy, like a show home, not a real home...and those random piles of ash she keeps in saucers. That's kinda weird."

"You noticed them too? You don't think Mary's...well...do you think the ash could be...?" Carol faltered, unable to suggest Mary might be doing something illegal and dangerous.

Jimmy sniggered.

"You suggesting miserable Mary's getting high on illicit substances, Carol? Nah, I don't think so. Looked to me more like she was burning incense. Everyone's talking about how she's running herself into the ground. Maybe she's trying to meditate and relax."

"You're so right; it was incense! Silly me! That's such a relief."

True to her word, Carol rang the following afternoon. Too exhausted to say much, Mary promised, at Carol's urging, to look after herself. If anything, Mary felt weaker. Angrier too. Carol's an interfering busybody who needs bringing down.

#

Mary's temps left on time on Friday, full of praise for Carol's compassionate management. Not only had she been kind to miserable Mary, but she'd secured contracts for most of them, either fixed-term or permanent, to replace those who were recovering or had died from the mystery food poisoning.

Carol and the bosses had lingered before deciding to meet up in the bar across the road. They all crowded into the same elevator, continuing the conversation about Mary's impressive proposals. They had decided to promote her and give her a private office space on her return to work. This meeting in the bar was an early celebration. Carol planned to phone Mary over the weekend and share the good news. She hoped it would speed Mary's recovery.

The lift clanged to a grinding halt between floors. The lights flickered out, and the conversation faltered to a stop. Carol shined her phone torch towards the control panel.

"Press the emergency button; someone will come soon."

The wail of the emergency siren competed with stifled screams as the car plummeted a short distance. Loud, metallic groans and creaks struck fear into everyone's heart. The lift jerked again. Carol and her companions lurched wildly, grabbing onto one another.

"Hello, lift number two! This is Jimmy from maintenance. Who's there? Is there a problem?"

"Jimmy? Jimmy, it's me, Carol, from yesterday. Hi, yeah, we've got a problem. Our lift is stuck. It's dropped a couple of times, but now it's stuck again. Can you help us?"

#

Mary's sleep was far from restful. Claustrophobia grabbed her by the throat. She pushed away the covers and gasped for air. She felt trapped. She couldn't see, but she could hear her own panicked breathing. The darkness swirled around her, a vicious entity seeking fresh victims. Mary's heart raced, then crashed to a stop. The thought bubbles swelled before losing animation. Mary's terror-filled dead eyes stared into the darkness. Thought bubble dust formed her shroud.

#

"Okay, Carol, I need you to stay calm for me. It'd be easier for everyone if you could turn off the alarm. Can you do that? Pull the emergency button back out."

A white-faced man nearest the panel fumbled in the dark, found the button, and yanked hard. The ensuing silence was a balm. He smiled in the dark and nodded in Carol's direction.

"Well done, guys, that's better. Okay, then, the fire crew have arrived ahead of the elevator techs. They've shut down the power, so your car won't move now. You're all doing okay, right? Right. We need to know how many of you are in there."

"Erm, hold on, let me double check. Okay, guys? Call out your names so I can get a number for the firemen."

Including herself, there were seven people trapped in the elevator. Carol reported the numbers back to Jimmy, who kept up a comforting rumble of conversation, keeping everyone calm.

"You're gonna hear someone thumping around up there shortly. The firies are gonna locate exactly where you are. We need to know which floor you're closest to, to decide the best way to get you all out. Hang on a sec, someone's telling me...yeah...okay...Carol? Carol, yeah, I'm back. Okay, right, we know exactly where you are now. You're gonna hear a lot of noise. It's okay, someone will enter the shaft above you and open the access panel in the car's ceiling. It'll be noisy, but you're all quite safe, okay?"

"Okay, Jimmy. Thanks. We can hear them!"

Although expected, the thumping and grinding was still nerve-wracking. A torch-lit face appeared grinning above them. Seven breaths were expelled simultaneously.

"You must be Carol. Hi, I'm Ben. Behind me here is John. I'm coming in; make some room. I'll help you put on a harness, and John will hoist you up and help you to the floor above. Dave will help you out, into the lobby. All you guys have to do is follow our instructions. You'll be out in no time." Ben grinned again and lowered himself into the car.

"Ladies first."

Ben strapped a harness under Carol's arms and lifted her up to the access door. John took up the slack and hauled her up and out of sight. The men could hear multiple voices. There was a whole team helping them. One by one, they donned the harness, and John hauled them to safety. By the time Ben surfaced, everyone was slumped against the lobby walls or sitting on the floor. Jimmy from maintenance had rustled up a tray of coffees.

"Lady and gentlemen, gather your belongings. We've eight flights of stairs to get down. It makes my job much easier if you can all stay together."

"Eight flights? Sir, I don't think Carol can manage that. She sprained her ankle..."

"Well, Carol, we can put you on a stretcher, no problem, or we could carry you?"

Blushing furiously, Carol protested she'd be fine and refused any assistance. Ben stayed close beside her all the way, allowing her to set the pace. When they reached the foyer, they noticed the out-of-order sign on lift number two and the small team of technicians who had arrived to fix the fault. Everyone spread out and milled around aimlessly, unsure what to do next.

"Are we still on? The bar's open, and I could really use a drink," said Carol.

Everyone flocked to her, grateful she had voiced their thoughts. Once settled in the bar, the conversation inevitably returned to Mary. Everyone agreed that when she came back to work, they'd have a real celebration. Her proposals had impressed everyone, and it would be to the company's advantage to make better use of her skills.

Ben barged into the bar, head turning frantically to find Carol. He called her name, and she waved. People moved out of his way, clearing a path between them.

"We found these in the elevator and the stairs. You must've snapped the string getting out of the elevator." He thrust a handful of beautiful pearlescent beads at her. They appeared to pulse and hum.

"But...they're not mine."

Ben looked at the pearly beads, then at Carol.

"I think they must be yours. Look," he nudged a solitary bead next to Carol's glass. "See? You lost another one. They obviously belong to you."

Jackson's Machine

by Melissa Quitadamo

"You like to upset me. You really do," Mary Howell said to her son.

She stood inside the screened walls of their back patio and sipped her third cup of tea. She scowled at the chrome-and-black motorcycle on display in the grass.

Jackson sat in his dirty armchair, his feet elevated and his head back. He rested his greasy jet-black hair on a floral pillow. The radio whistled beside him, its antennas pointing at odd angles and the Phillies game indiscernible through static.

Mary glanced sideways up at the dark windows of the neighboring houses.

"People talk, you know," she said.

"Who cares what people think?" he mumbled.

"A child's behavior is a reflection on their mother."

"I'm not a child."

She twisted the pearls around her neck with her forefinger. "I'll never leave the house again."

Dark clouds appeared on the horizon.

"I'm sure it will rain," she said.

Jackson leaned forward to adjust the antennas.

"No, no, Dear! Let me. You've never been good at these things." Jackson sat back again, and Mary rushed over to the radio.

"All children like to torment their mothers these days. They have no respect for their mother's hearts." She jerked the metal sticks this way and that.

The whistling stopped, and the announcer's voice came through.

"Thanks, Ma."

"Of course, Sweetie."

He folded his fingers together on his stomach and closed his eyes.

Mary leaned forward, stroked her son's hair once, and resumed her place at the screen. In the yard, her laundry hung on the line—colorful socks, shirts, nightgowns, and pants swayed.

She slurped from her cup, sucking the tea between her teeth.

"Bad enough you risk your own life on such a machine, let alone hers."

Jackson's eyelids drooped.

"Jackson!"

"Ma!" He folded his arms in protest.

"Just one slip on the pavement, and her head will crack like a little egg!"

"I'll give her my helmet."

Mary snorted and sucked in her bottom lip.

"And what about your poor little head, Jack."

Jackson sank deep into the cushions. He closed his eyes and smacked his lips.

Mary set her teacup down and turned to the tin of cookies laid to rest on the patio table.

"You never know what could happen." She popped the lid off the tin.

Jackson cracked open an eye and glanced at the cookies, so buttery and sweet, which filled the house with their fragrance that morning.

"All these new machines are so dangerous now."

Tin in hand, she slinked over to her son's chair. "All the other women in this neighborhood go down to the laundromat, you know. Women all across America go down to their laundromats. But it's no good, I tell you, no good. Never a day goes by I don't hear of one woman or other being electrocuted when they push the buttons on those machines. Affects their brains and all that. But not me. Give me a washboard and basin any day."

She held the tin over him. He smelled the cookies, so crisp and sweet. He reached out.

"Just today, Mrs. Bishop told me of her nephew." She spun around before he grabbed one. "What was his name? Greg. Craig. Something, no matter. Her nephew drove on one of those godforsaken four-lane highways—with his wife and their baby in the car. Well, wouldn't you know, cars came this way and went that way at such a speed you wouldn't believe. They'd only gotten as far as Reading when another car clipped the side of them. They careened off the road, turned, and flipped down a ravine. He was thrust into the windshield, she was thrown out the window, and I needn't tell you the baby didn't make it."

Jackson watched the tin jolt around in her hand.

"I needn't tell you not a one of them survived. Imagine, just imagine, a three-person funeral—and one of them a baby. And they placed that poor child in the arms of her mother, dressed in her christening outfit. She never even made it to her christening, Jack." Her voice was all aquiver as she lifted her free hand over her eyes.

"Ah, Ma, don't cry."

She parted her fingers and peeked between them. He looked up at her, his eyebrows scrunched and lips puckered.

"It's just, you like to upset me. You really do," she whimpered.

"I'm sorry, Ma. Really, I am. Don't cry."

She wiped her eyes with the back of her hand and cleared her throat.

"You know I love you, more than life itself. I've been so lonely since your father died. Imagine the horror if I learn you've perished in an accident—your body parts all twisted and broken. I pray the good Lord takes me before I lose you too." She sniffed hard, bent over, and kissed her son on the forehead.

She lowered the tin.

Jackson grabbed half a dozen cookies.

He lifted a cookie to his mouth.

"Heavens above!" She tossed the tin on the table and set to smacking him hard on the arm with the back of her hand.

Through the screen, she'd spotted a black man walking down the street.

"Look, look," she hissed, never taking her eyes off the stranger.

"Ma!" he whined. Bits of mushy crumbs fell from his mouth.

"Look, look!" She pointed.

He sat up, now surrendering both his cookies and his nap. He glanced through the screen. The man wore a white uniform and white cap on his head. In his hands, he carried a case of milk bottles and walked toward their house. Jackson turned back, closed his eyes, and pinched the bridge of his nose.

"He's delivering milk, Ma."

"Oh, you think so, do you?"

Mary craned her neck and squinted through the screen.

"He's not our milkman. Joseph Turner has delivered my milk to me every day for the past ten years."

"Old Joe is probably just sick—or on vacation."

"Oh, Jack, how naïve you are. Poor Joe is dead, and this man murdered him."

"For what purpose, Ma? To steal his milk?" Jackson tossed his uneaten cookies back into the tin with a clang.

"Who knows, but he's an imposter. He's murdered Joe, stole his uniform and truck, and now he's come to murder me too!"

"Don't overexcite yourself."

A hard knock rapped on the front door.

"This is it, he's coming for us, Jack!"

Jackson stood and went into the house.

"Take care! Take care!"

Jackson returned a moment later with a bottle of milk in hand.

"See, Ma, milk." He grinned and raised the bottle to his lips.

Mary snatched the bottle from his hand, opened the patio door, and poured it out.

Jackson watched the steady stream of white liquid drain from the bottle into the grass below.

"Whad'ya do that for, Ma?" He asked through clenched teeth.

"He's poisoned it, I'm sure of it."

Jackson rolled his eyes.

"Don't roll your eyes at me; they'll get stuck! I saw a man the other day, about your age, bagging my groceries, and each eye went in different directions. No doubt he rolled his eyes a time or two too many at his mother."

Jackson groaned and rubbed his hand across his face.

"Alright, Ma, I gotta get going!"

"And you'll leave me here, all alone, while murderers roam the streets? He's waiting for you to leave so he can come back for me!"

Jackson retreated into the house.

Mary turned away and stared hateful at his bike again.

The sun disappeared altogether, and she looked into the sky, now veiled in gray. She glimpsed a quick streak of blue—a flash—but it was instantaneous and far away on the horizon. Perhaps it was lightning or just one of the bright spotlights from the theater.

Jackson returned to the porch wearing his leather jacket and black boots.

"I'm sure it will rain and you'll be soaked through. You'll skid off the road, slam into a tree, and break every bone in your body." She grabbed hold of his collar and pulled him in. "You can't leave now. Look at the sky!"

"That's why I gotta go, Ma! The sooner I leave, the better." He grabbed hold of her wrists and pulled her clawing hands off his jacket.

He leaned in and kissed her once on the cheek.

Mary held her hands to her mouth and whimpered.

Jackson walked across the lawn to his bike and climbed on.

"I know you think I'm overbearing!" she shouted after him. "When you're my age, you'll understand. When you have children, I hope they're just like you, so you know what I put up with and—" Her voice was drowned out by the thundering of his bike.

He made a half circle in the grass, exited the yard, and sped down the street.

She watched him as far as the bend until he disappeared between a cluster of trees, and she knew he wouldn't return.

"This is just a phase. It'll pass. All children go through their little rebellions. He'll come back to me in the end."

She heard a soft rumble above. She knew it would rain.

The laundry whipped flag-like in the quickening breeze.

What would the neighbors think of her? She glanced over at the houses and imagined she saw the shadows of people passing back and forth between the frames. They watched her, laughed at her.

"I'm a good mother," Mary whispered.

She grabbed her straw basket, pushed open the door, and rushed down the stairs and into the yard. At the line, she pulled off wooden pins in a frenzy and threw shirts and socks and nightgowns and pants into a heap. When she'd nearly finished, she heard a loud crack above her head. Everything turned bright, and her body filled with intense heat. She slowed, became rigid, and fell.

Then it was dark, and Mary lay dead in the grass.

The hem of her skirt was on fire, only extinguished by rapid rainfall. Smoke rose from her body in the cool air. Her pearls deteriorated into bits of flaking ash around her neck. Along her jaw, where the lightning struck, her veins turned bright red beneath her white skin.

Her wide eyes reflected the gray sky, and her lips parted into the slightest smile.

The Pleiades

by Jerine Pace-Watson

They were five, gathered together. And they waited. Soft, muted sobs escaped from them now and again, and they occasionally dabbed at their moist redness with small, white, cottony balls.

Shutter couldn't sit still. She kept lifting her feet, one after the other, and wringing two of her hands. Her nervous agitation irritated her sisters, and her constant movement made the floor tremble.

"For Weaver's sake, Shutter! Be still! We've got enough trouble as it is without being bounced up and down like a bunch of common Long-Legs!"

"I'm sorry, Scythe. It's just that...I can't believe she's dead! She was so young! With so much to live for! Why doesn't Silo get here? She's never on time for anything!"

"She's too damned fat, that's why. She can't move fast enough. She never should've wound up near all that grain."

Quick to criticize, Sugar Cane was sleek and vain. She was the only sister living in the remote wilderness, and the rugged environment had honed her body into a lean hardness. She had also grown callous and intolerant.

"Shut up, Sugar. All I've heard since I got here was how YOU lived the farthest away, how YOU arrived first, and how YOU can't stay long because it's harvest time. You, you, you! Our baby sister has been killed, and you sit there thinking only of your selfish self!"

"I'm not selfish, Shutter. I'm smart. And careful. If September had been half as careful, she wouldn't be dead. And we wouldn't have had to stop everything for this stupid meeting, and I could be getting my food while it's fresh."

"Alright. Hush. That's enough. I won't stand for any more bickering. Besides, I think I feel Silo coming."

Shingle's voice carried a note of quiet authority. She was the oldest of the sisters and in command. With the wisdom of her maturity, she made all of the family's decisions, and her judgment was never questioned. She glared a warning at Sugar Cane as Silo ponderously tried to heave herself up and through the lace-like camouflage draped over the opening.

Suddenly, Shutter shrieked as Silo lost her foothold and began to slip. Throwing her a lifeline before anyone else thought to move, Stirrup leaned fearlessly out over the chasm, pulling Silo into the safety of the cave.

"Thank you, Stirrup. Whew, what a climb! Is it true? Is...is September really dead?"

Silo clutched her shiny breast as her five sisters nodded a sad affirmation. Her breath jerked out in spasms as she sobbed into her dingy gray ball. In her anxious haste, she had dragged it behind her, all the way from the grain bin.

Silo was even more insecure than Shutter. Ever since Chimney, their mother, had perished in a freak downdraft, Silo had become more and more fearful. She rarely ventured anywhere anymore, staying at home, curled tightly inward, consoling herself with too much food.

Shingle sidled over to Silo and stroked her plump blackness in four places at once, until her heaving sobs dissolved into watery sniffles. Clicking her mandibles soothingly, Shingle rocked her plump sister to and fro, looking at the other sisters over Silo's black head.

"There, there, now. Sweet Silo. We all know September was your special joy. You must try to remember she loved you too. You were her favorite sister, and we all knew it. You gave her so much happiness."

"Oh, I know, Shing, I know. But she was such a sweet, dainty little thing. I knew in my insides something was wrong, even before I got the Wire-Throb. She was supposed to have come for dinner two nights ago. I had fixed her favorite, Fritillary with Greenbottle dressing. When she didn't show up, I was so upset, I ate the whole thing. Then I got worried sick and waited past Dew Time at the Wire End. I didn't get the Wire-Throb until the next day, and besides, the stupid Hopper was drunk on tobacco juice and got the message all garbled. That's why I wasn't sure whether or not she was...she was...oh, I can't even say it! How did it happen? What got her? The Tab? A Beak? A swarm of Hummers?"

"No, dear, none of those. You had trained her very well. It was no fault of yours."

The other sisters, even Sugar Cane, acknowledged Shingle's statement with nods and clicks. They moved closer in order to stroke Silo, exchanging guilty looks among themselves.

Many Glow-Darks earlier, when September had newly emerged, Chimney had asked each of her older daughters to teach the Patterns to their new baby sister. Chimney had grown too old, she said, to remember all the details of the Early Windings, much less the basic rules for survival. Stirrup, Shutter, Sugar Cane, Scythe, and even Shingle had all been too busy holding the threads of their own lives together and had refused to help. But not Silo. She had agreed immediately, without hesitation, taking

September home with her that very day. Silo's own daughters had long since grown and gone into their own Sisterlife, and she was lonely.

September proved a deft weaver, memorizing the ancient Patterns rapidly, emitting cheerful musical clicks as she worked her way through the Hexagon, the Septagon, and the Octagon. Silo would sit nearby, eating constantly, smiling with encouragement as her little sister strained to remember the intricacies of their heritage. When September had finally mastered the difficult Double Decagon, Silo taught her the Second Phase: avoiding the Hummers, the Beaks, and the evil, furry Tab. September had listened respectfully, absorbing all that Silo had ever known.

Her training program had been the highlight of Silo's life, even more memorable than her own Wedding Feast Day, though she dared not tell anyone that. To Silo, the long-awaited Wedding Feast had been a bit of a disappointment. All that build-up, and then it was over in an instant. In contrast, all the Dawns and Darks spent teaching September had stretched on and on in pleasurable companionship, and Silo remembered each single moment with nostalgia.

"What, then? What happened to her?" Silo's voice choked with new tears as she looked to Shingle for an answer.

"That's why I Wire-Throbbed everyone to come here. All of us are needed."

Shingle drew herself up tall, stiffening her cephalothorax for emphasis. "It was an unprovoked, unwarranted attack from an enemy heretofore unsuspected. The FarmWoman killed her, Silo!"

"The FarmWoman? You must be mistaken! Why, just the other day, she thundered near me, and I didn't even drop a stitch! She's never been a threat before!"

"Shing is right. I saw it happen." Stirrup's nasal whine was tremulous.

"Go ahead, Stirrup," Shingle prodded. "Tell Silo what you've told us."

Silo clutched her black breast again, her eight eyes oscillating with terror. Stirrup paused, glancing at her feet, then began her story.

"It was early, very early. The Dark was not quite gone. For some reason, I had waked up earlier than usual. That was the day the Choke Wind blew in, and I guess the noise of the tack room door—slamming and slamming—woke me up. It sounded like ten thousand Rainmakers. Anyway, I hurried to my old Pattern to drink the dew before it blew away. The next thing I knew, I had finished my new Pattern in record time, and I decided to go see how September was doing. Poor thing. It's a shame none of us changed her name after she emerged. If only we had realized that Chimney must have been senile, giving her a nomadic name like 'September.' Maybe, with another name, she wouldn't have patterned so aimlessly and been so…vulnerable."

"Get on with it, Stirrup!" Shingle had begun to pat her feet, all of them, impatiently. She was very wise, but she did not share the limelight easily.

"Ah. Yes. Well, as I remember it, the Choke Wind made walking terribly precarious, and I had to use double pulley strands, even in the grass. It took forever to work my way over to Porch Place, but at least I was out of the wind when I got there. I could see September, high up, near the left eave. She was dangerously close to the Squeak Swing, again. Evidently, she had just waked up and was still dew drinking. She hadn't started her new Pattern and didn't see me coming up the Post Road. I was thinking what a nice surprise my visit would be, and I could even help her with her Pattern. I was going to suggest, tactfully of course, a safer place. The right eave, maybe..."

"Yes, yes, Stirrup! We aren't questioning your intentions! But you are digressing as usual, and we don't have much time!" Shingle was making an effort not to lose her temper, and all of the sisters were beginning to tremble.

Stirrup's feelings were hurt. She clicked her pedipalpi petulantly, abstractedly winding her floss around three of her hands, bristling at each of her sisters in turn.

"None of you seems to realize how painful this is for me. I'm trying very, very hard to tell it absolutely straight and factual. It was a traumatic experience. I'm lucky to be alive, let me tell you!"

No one said another word. Stirrup was determined to take all the time she felt necessary, regardless of anyone's opinion, even Shingle's.

"Alright, then. Well. Like I was saying, I was halfway up the Post Road, intent upon surprising September, when the Wood Wall opened and a big cloud of Peachtree Smell wafted over me. I stopped climbing just to enjoy it before it dissipated, as we all do, when all of a sudden, I heard a roaring sound...no, it was more of an explosion, really. It seemed to be coming from the Pink Grinding Pouch in FarmWoman's head. She had come from behind the Wood Wall and had folded herself down onto the Squeak Swing. Then she lunged upright, thundered back through the Wood Wall, and slammed it back together so violently, the entire Post Road quaked and I almost fell off! By the time I had secured my line, the Wood Wall opened again, and FarmWoman never gave September a chance! I looked up in time to see the little dear falling from her Pattern, a shiny dew drop still on her mandibles. Her line was out, but she was obviously caught off guard because her Free Fall was too long. Then, just as she started back up, FarmWoman shot her. Dead."

"Shot her?" Silo was incredulous.

"Yes. Shot her. With a Vapor Dart Cannon! Millions of volleys! Enough to kill a hundred of us! If a lucky gust from the Choke Wind hadn't blown most of the vapor away, it would've killed me too! I couldn't even risk dragging her body away. I couldn't get that close! The odor was noxious. And that's all I saw. I ran straight up to Shingle's Pattern after that. Poor little thing! Her legs! They were curled so horribly!"

Stirrup sobbed into her threads, now grown into a large, cottony ball. The sisters wept anew at the end of the tale, each visualizing the death scene, each fearful of the same fate. Scythe was the first to comment, her didactic monotone somewhat subdued by her grief.

"Our great-grandmother died the same way. Chimney told me about it."

"Scythe is right. I'd forgotten." Shingle nodded, acknowledging Scythe's sharp memory.

"Lampshade was her name, remember?" Scythe continued as the sisters clicked in yesses. "She emerged in the Inner World and lived a long time, considering the dangers there. But FarmWoman didn't shoot her with the Vapor Darts. FarmMan did. And before the sisters could dispense with him, he left in the Long Box."

"Scythe is correct." Shingle asserted herself, taking control of the conversation once again. "At the conclave after Lampshade's death, it was decided Lampshade must have avenged herself in her final agony. At any rate, the Long Box swallowed FarmMan whole. He never came back to fix the tack room door or to cut the cane. We voted to forgive FarmWoman for the murder committed by her mate. We truly wanted to live peacefully near her—because, after all, she is a female of her species, as strange as she looks; and, before this, she had never lifted a Flesh Fan against any of us. For this reason, it was agreed that even a creature as hideously cumbersome and ignorant as FarmWoman should be allowed to exist. The sisters thought surely plain common sense would have taught her to respect us. But now, she has killed our beloved September."

Shingle paused, drew in a deep breath, and lowered her voice. "By the power invested in all who wear the Crimson Carapace, we do now declare, in this, the Conclave of September, all past decisions null and void. FarmWoman must die. The sentence is to be carried out immediately."

All of Shingle's eight eyes glittered in the dimness. The six surviving sisters clustered together as Shingle explained the Death Plan. There were objections and questions lasting long into the Dark, but in the end, even Shutter found the courage to agree. Knowing they would either succeed and live or all die together, they solemnly made their way up the Wood

Wall, over the eave where September's last Pattern hung tattered and empty, all the way to the great height of Shingle's Pattern.

After resting briefly, they divided into pairs, as designated by the Death Plan. Shingle and Silo took up the lead. Silo would never have been able to keep up otherwise. Next in line crept Scythe and Shutter. Shutter's trembling was visibly uncontrollable, and she could not have participated except from the most protected position. Stirrup and Sugar Cane, the strongest fighters, brought up the rear flank.

Up, up they climbed, past Shingle's Pattern, struggling with the steep angle of the incline and a strong headwind. At a signal from Shingle, who knew every inch of this terrain, they coiled their ropes at the base of a shiny vent pipe near the uppermost peak. They began to scale the slick metal protuberance, climbing on top of each other in turn until Stirrup reached the top and dropped a line down inside the silver-colored cylinder. From then on, their invasion into the Inner World was less difficult. Getting out after the deed was done would present a problem, but they tried not to think of that. Earlier Shingle had reassured them, pointing out that there would be no need for haste afterward if their mission was successful. The "if" bothered Shutter frightfully, but she knew nothing could alter a Death Plan.

They had dropped through the round tin opening, down into The Musty Place full of The Patterns of the Ancients, and it was just as Shingle had described. Gossamer dust clung to everything, but The Musty Place had sheltered their predecessors from weather. Every innovation in stitching had been perfectly preserved. Scythe longed to linger and study the relics. Some of the old Patterns she had never even heard of, much less seen.

Ahead of the others, Shingle held up all four hands, signaling them to stop. In front of her was a narrow opening, cut in a square around a loosely fitting trap door. Soft, warm air wafted upward from the crack.

"We have to drop down from this opening, and it's a long way. This is it. The Inner World. Get your spinnerets ready."

Silo had trouble wedging herself through the crack, but with a well-placed kick from Sugar Cane and a shove from Stirrup, she oozed through and disappeared in a breathtaking downward plunge. The others followed in rapid succession, and all but Shingle were startled by the strangeness of the landing surface.

"What is this? What are we walking on?"

"I guess it's Inner World grass, Shutter, but it doesn't grow."

"I don't like it, Shingle. It sticks to my feet and feels dead!"

"Scythe, get back in line and shut her up. We don't have much more Dark left, and we're not the least bit interested in her sticky feet."

Shingle led them on through the cavernous nothingness, skirting slick trunks that sprouted no leaves and apparently had no roots. The lifeless growth underfoot ended abruptly, and they stumbled through a fuzzy patch of long strands that seemed to grow inexplicably from the edge of the dead grass. Working their way along, they skittered across a large open area of the slickest wood they had ever touched. Shutter, more frightened than ever, slipped down; but Scythe, close beside her, helped her up before anyone noticed.

Now they were in the FarmWoman's Cave. They could hear her loud Sleep Breathing; it sounded like a Giant Hummer, pulsating weirdly, deafening them with its vibrations. Silo whimpered and clung to Shingle.

"Hurry. In here." Shingle pointed one hand.

In a frenzied scramble, their book lungs bursting, the sisters hid under an inside Wood Wall and bumped and tumbled over each other on the opposite side.

"This is it. We made it!" Shingle's whisper sounded too loud in the darkness.

"Where are we, Shing?" croaked Scythe.

"Right where I told you we'd have to be, when I outlined the Plan. This is where FarmWoman keeps her Walk Feet. See? Here's one. Feel it. It's soft. Like our winding balls."

Shutter and Silo stretched up quivering hands to feel the texture of the fabric.

"I still don't know how you can be so sure this will work." Sugar Cane was getting dubious.

"You'll just have to trust me, Sugar," said Shingle. "When I spent so many Dawns and Darks here in the Inner World long ago, I watched and I learned. FarmWoman puts her hind legs in these, every Dawn, and never looks down. Now, climb inside this one, all of you. Go on, get way up into the darkest part. Squeeze up, close together. That's it. We're going to do it! You'll see!"

The sisters obediently hid themselves far up into the low-ceilinged, foul-smelling place. They were six, gathered together. And they waited.

* * *

From the Sunday NEWS-GAZETTE:

"George Swenson's widow was found dead Saturday morning in the bedroom of her modest farmhouse. A neighbor, Mrs. James Morehouse, said she had telephoned Mrs. Swenson the night before, and they discussed going to the County Fair together on Saturday. Mrs. Swenson was clad in her nightclothes, wearing only one house shoe. There were no signs of violence, but an autopsy has been ordered. Funeral arrangements will be announced."

From the Tuesday evening GAZETTE:

"The coroner's office reports Mrs. Ella Euline Swenson died as a result of multiple black widow spider bites, six to be exact. All were inflicted on the left foot, a most unusual occurrence. Mrs. Swenson was the widow of George Swenson, who died only last February. She will be remembered fondly for her homemade peach fritters, a favorite of past county fairs. She is survived by one daughter, Mrs. Christine Templeton of Tampa, and one son, Seaman First Class George Swenson Jr., stationed in Norfolk, Virginia. Funeral arrangements are pending. Final-Rest Funeral Parlor."

From the Monday morning NEWS:

FOR SALE. DIAMOND-IN-THE-ROUGH.

"Small farm, 122 ac., cane, sorghum, harvest-ready. 2BR, 1B frame house, wood shingle roof, attic storage. Stove, ref., porch swing, storm shutters; tack room, barn, silo need repairs. Tractor, tools, old saddle included. Wire fence around property. For relaxed country living, call JIM or OPAL, MOREHOUSE REALTY, 771-2994

Life After Birth

by Lucy Merriman

One.

I knocked on the side of the bathroom stall. I was squatting so as not to touch my skin to the public toilet seat, even though rationally I knew it was clean. The entire room smelled like citrus and bleach, which I guess is better than smelling like feces? It always makes my eyes sting though. But anyway, that's why I always take a bathroom break at 3:12, because it's right after the bathroom is cleaned. Near enough that nobody else has used it yet, but long enough that I won't run into the janitor. I still don't want to sit down though.

Anyway, Bella Cholle does the same thing, same time, and she's the only other person I trust here. I don't like her, exactly? But I trust her. And somebody needed to know. She knocked back.

"What do you want, Rainy?" she asked. Not unkindly; she's just to-the-point like that. I sucked in a deep breath.

"I accidentally rebooted someone," I said in a rush, running my fingertips along my naked thighs. "His name is Steven Hall, he's 89, and, well now he's not 89, if you get what I mean. I'm not really sure how to go about reporting it. Or, um, undoing it?" I could feel my heart catch in my throat. The stall door seemed to be leaning toward me, and I wanted to pull up my knees, but that would mean touching the toilet seat, which abruptly seemed perilously close. I balled my hand into a fist and pressed against my abdomen, forcing an exhale. "I do know how to report it actually, I do. I just don't want to. I can't lose this job, Bella. I've lost so many, I…"

"He didn't run through the scheduled shutdown first?"

"No."

I clenched my eyes shut to keep from crying. My voice didn't quaver this time. "He was supposed to run for thirty more cycles, and, you know. And there's not even a body." My hamstrings began to tremble from the prolonged squat, and I didn't know if I could manage to squat and confess and pee all at once; something was going to give. Part of me desperately wanted to pull up my slacks and bolt out of there, but that'd mean I couldn't pee until I got home, because somebody would definitely use the stall in the meantime.

Bella was peeing fine. After she was done, when I heard her fiddling with the toilet paper roll, I managed to ask, you know: "What should I do?"

"How did you even—aren't you in the design department?" she asked. "How could you reboot without a password? You're not remotely authorized—"

"I don't know," I moaned, a timid trickle of urine finally leaking into the bowl. I ran my hand through my hair. This needed to happen, but now it needed to be over.

"I'll take care of it," Bella said. I heard the door to her stall swing open too fast and clatter against the wall. I flinched, but of course she didn't see me, and I watched through the gap under the door as she clicked her way to a sink in her black stilettos. I focused on the sound of running water and closed my eyes again.

"Bella?" I asked. "How are you going to take care of it?"

The water sounds stopped. "Efficiently," is all she said. And then she left.

I did too, but not until 3:28.

When I returned to my cubicle, my computer was open to a folder of preliminary artwork for a new module, and I'd missed a call from Dr. Platt, my direct supervisor. I was afraid it had been about what I'd told Bella, but it turns out he just wanted my input on some new paperwork designs. I kept waiting for anyone to ask me about Steven Hall or for a memo to go around about his disappearance—or, more likely, something about a patch to fix an error that was vaguely, yet sinisterly, termed.

I kept waiting.

After four months, I was fired because I was supposed to bring the coffee, and I'd mixed up Janet Hilk's Caramel Frappuccino with Dr. Platt's hazelnut one, which wouldn't be a big deal except that Janet is allergic to all nuts, so she swole up and stopped breathing. While it could not have been lethal, as Janet has 68 cycles to go, her asphyxiation caused a worrying 503 Error for quite some time on all of her system's pages, which lasted until she was successfully intubated by paramedics. So, she was really upset.

Plus, as she and many people yelled all at once, Janet's tree-nut allergy is a well-known FACT, and was I a MURDERER at heart?

I am not a murderer. I was just bad at my job, which is why it's not my job anymore.

Two.

A Letter of Assessment Regarding the Repercussions of the Unscheduled Reboot of Steven Hall.

Dear Chairman Martinez,

It has been determined by the Committee on Human and Technological Error that the error causing the unscheduled reboot of Steven Hall was primarily human in nature. However, the probability of this reboot resulting disaster is low, <0.0012%. Steven Hall's disappearance will primarily cause familial and communal anxiety in twenty-three relatives for less than one year, followed by predictable grief responses over the next five years.

In only two relatives will this grief likely resolve into a profound unsettlement, a restlessness that will cause them to wander, fall in and out of love too quickly, lose money, and make art. One is now significantly likely to become fat when she would've been slender, and because of this, she marries a different man, thus diverting her from the optimized life course. However, as she will have no children, this will be moot within a generation.

While long-term effect is unlikely, it is recommended that all passwords to access programming changes be altered due to potential breach.

Sincerely,

Bella Cholle

Dir. of Department of Disaster

Humanity LLC

As she hit "send" on her report, Bella focused her attention on the palm on her left hand, which she studiously relaxed.

She never missed the old days, the days before we knew the nature of reality and wondered just who's in charge of this whole mess. She never missed imagining it was a wise and compassionate God (whose existence, priests argue, isn't technically ruled out by our current understanding of

The Algorithm), nor did she regret the formation of Humanity LLC, the corporation made to wind the intergalactic pocket watch of physical space—and everyone in it.

If she regretted a life of brutal calculation—one spent balancing the needs of the people as a whole with the wants of the highest bidders—if she regretted her own quest for revelation at the expense of certainty of her own free will, if she felt a prickle of nostalgia behind her eyes, it didn't show.

No. The air was cleaner now; people—in general—healthier, happier, more okay. Bella Cholle was more okay.

For the fifth time today, she pulled up Rainy Ellis's personal page. Refreshed it. Watched the heart rate monitor blip, even-toned, watched statistics shuffle around. Re-read Rainy's relationship projections. Good. Good.

This is how okay people spend their day.

Three.

Steven had been a loner for his last thirty years on Earth, albeit an amiable one. After scattering his wife's ashes in the apple orchard—patting the last of her carbon into the mulch, overturning the dirt until his palms were caked with brown instead of gray—he walked. Didn't walk back to the house either. Just...walked.

He'd found himself lighter than he'd expected; all while she died, her love for him—and his as well—pooled in dammed veins around his heart and made heavy weights around his ankles. He couldn't have known that he cradled the dying love in the folds of his skin as tenderly as he cradled the woman he loved in his arms. So, when the love stood up to leave, he was enlightened.

As he was walking for thirty years, Steven found himself amused by everyone he met, enjoying company without any desire to keep it.

So, too, did he experience the deep caverns he explored as he walked: sans judgment. With their glowing fauna and blind white fish, each one smelled like the limestone cellars of his childhood. He once watched a fruit bat flock careen along the horizon line in a chaotic, clicking euphony. He enjoyed them too. He didn't love them.

He would've kept walking forever, but one morning he stepped out of his tent and across the threshold of life and death: from a dry, arid darkness to a damp one.

His wife's death had happened right on schedule; his own was unexpected. But, as he pieced it together—the darkness, the warmth, the taut of his skin, the perfect-circle-ness of his body—he accepted this pretty well too.

His life before birth was quiet for the first few months. He'd earned a rest.

Eventually, his rest was disrupted.

He heard the fetus-songs.

There are many things about life in the womb that are hard to describe. "Fetus-songs pass through the membranes of cells." "Fetus-songs travel from skin to skin when the golgi apparatus vibrates." Neither of these things are anywhere near correct. Born people can never hear them. Born people will never know that they hear each other, let alone why.

Steven Hall was as close to born as anyone who's heard the fetus-songs ever would be, and he could hardly bear it. They made him so sad.

Here is how the stories of fetuses are: they are about darkness, wetness, and warmth. They are about patches of grey and white, about blood and oxygen, about the joy of feeling your fingers grow and running them against the walls of The Womb. They have hundreds of words for these feelings, words that we wouldn't know as words, for they speak in the intermingling manner of dreams.

Fetuses speak of sudden coldness, sudden twinness, of music and bones. Fetus stories are about each other; they are about love, for they do love one another; they are about The Mother, who is mysterious and beautiful and is either whole and all or nothing; they are about birth.

Fetuses fear birth most of all.

The fear of birth is a primal thing. There is a scabbling about it, an avoidance of it, for it is such a sad thing. But what could be done about it? A life is nine months long, and then you disappear. The Womb, your home, rejects you. Your mind is vanished from the landscape. You are mourned. You are gone. This fear crackles 'round the edges of every experience, every daydream, like static on the skin.

Steven Hall listened for two whole months to their conversation. He tried to accept it. He tried to feel amused. But Steven Hall was not an old man anymore. He had lost his patience and was gaining on his love again, so about the fifty thousandth time he heard the whimpering at the shadows, he blurted: "It's not like that!"

He almost clapped his hand over his mouth, startled as he was to hear his voice in this place. Of course, it wasn't his voice, wasn't his larynx or his tongue that made the words, but they reverberated like a shout.

Life moves quickly when it's short, so while the other fetuses had noticed Steven, they hadn't the time to think of him. But, now he'd shouted.

They turned to him expectantly.

"It's just that you don't have to be so scared, that's all," he said lamely. "I've been there. Out there, I've been...born."

"And now I'm back here, and birth! Well, it's not so bad when you get down to it."

The other fetuses listened politely. Someone shy and far away asked hesitantly: "What's it like, then?" Her name in the fetus-song was Yesterday.

Steven floundered for the words. "Brighter. More...colors, fewer shadows. More people. Everyone becomes people, it's marvelous!" He clenched and opened his hands. "Tricky, that. There's sunlight, and it makes soft shadows under someone's nose and chin when it shines on them. And it casts long shadows behind them when they walk east in the morning."

"What are shadows?" another fetus asked, one with staccato dreams in red and orange.

"They're like echoes," Steven said. "But, for sight. Sight is a sense you gain

when you're born—well, usually. Most people. Sight is a way of experiencing objects and people, different than hearing or touching or...dreaming of."

"Sounds bad," whispered the fetus who dreamed in hot colors. The other fetuses murmured in agreement.

"No!" barked Steven. "It's good! Great, even." He grimaced at himself for barking. Why should it matter?

Why should he care to ease their fear a whit?

"I think you're making it up," said a third fetus, who was named Point in the song.

Yesterday nodded. "That's okay though. He can make things up if he wants to."

"Still," said Point, his thoughts drifting back to the song from earlier in the day. "Scary to lose someone so soon."

"I will miss Song-Song," said Yesterday. And, for that day, the fetuses did miss Song-Song, one of their own who was born before her time. Steven Hall was quiet for it.

The next day, mourning was over because fetuses' lives are short and their memories shorter, and again the cosmic dream-song became one of a small riverboat in a stormy sea.

The Mother hates us.

The Mother loves us.

The Mother gives us breath and food.

The Mother turns us all away, one by one by one.

The Mother made the blood-sack and dream-silk.

The Mother sometimes sings hello. She never sings goodbye.

No, The Mother never sings goodbye.

Again, Steven heard their songs, and he grieved with them, but shuddered too. Such pointless grief. And the pointlessness overwhelmed his limited compassion for the grieving strange, for his love was growing as he did, and it was becoming heavy.

So, in love, his anger on their behalf spilled onto them.

"The Mother sends us from her womb to hold us in her arms," he said.

The other fetuses stopped singing and glared at Steven's intrusion.

"No…?" the others said.

"'s true," Steven said sullenly. "And there are lots of mothers."

"That's ridiculous!" The fetus called Point exploded. "The Mother does not have arms!"

Meekly, Yesterday cleared her throat. "We don't know. She could have arms."

"There's no way she has arms," Point argued, as the song splintered and went jagged around them. "Why should she? Just because we have arms? Arms are weird and useless. The Mother doesn't need vestigial things like arms. They're good for holding your knees, but that's about it."

"Maybe she has arms because they're beautiful and she likes beautiful things?" suggested another, someone Steven hadn't heard before.

"Or," Yesterday wondered aloud, "maybe you meant The Mother has arms metaphorically?"

"I don't mean metaphorically, no," said Steven. Yesterday sighed. "Honestly. Look," Steven said, "I know because I've been there! Mothers have real arms. They hold you. It's wonderful."

"Er, wouldn't it be quite slimey if someone else touched you with their arms?" asked the new voice.

"Daydream, how are you still afraid of your own slime?" Yesterday demanded.

"You've been in your slime stage for fourteen days now. Get a grip."

"It's just that, if The Mother has arms, it would be double the slime, which might be more than I can handle."

"You'd be born," snapped Point. "You wouldn't handle anything. There'd be no 'you' left. You'd be cut out of the conversation, no exceptions."

"You are still you after birth, though," pleaded Steve.

"Enough of this!" The fetus-song became urgent, overlapping, fearful, and angry.

"Life after birth is real," Steven pressed, "and it can be scary, but it can also be beautiful. And so many people are mothers. My wife was a mother! We both held our son, and he was wonderful, and then he grew up—"

Stoney silence fell.

"Maybe he meant—" Yesterday tried to interject, but the renewed clamor of the fetuses drowned her out.

"LIAR."

"Why could someone become a mother? That doesn't make any sense."

"HERETIC! There is only one mother, The Mother of all of us—"

"I just don't understand what you think a mother is. Someone like us, sure, but someone with arms? Someone we could become? Does everyone have a secret hidden womb to grow people in?"

"STOP trying to make his ravings make SENSE. He's LYING."

"He just wants to make people feel better. Nothing wrong with that…"

"It's wrong and it's cruel. People have to grieve."

"I never said not to grieve," Steven tried to say, but nobody heard him.

The roar of the fetus-dream-song had turned icy and obsidian-dark, and there was nothing to do but wait until the cymbal clash was over. Everybody lost to birth was thrown down as evidence, every old wound reopened and drained into the water of the argument.

They fought for six days.

Then, all at once, they stopped.

Or, Steven couldn't hear them anymore, at least. It's difficult to explain what they did. Suffice it to say: they turned away from him.

It was a little while before anyone had heard anything again. But, a third of a life later, he heard Yesterday again.

"Steven?"

"Yes?"

"In the time after you were born, you and a mother had a son?"

"Yes, that's right," he said.

"What happened to him?"

"Oh," Steven said, puzzled. "What did happen to him? Well, let's see. He grew up, got married himself. No kids of his own. Trained dogs for a living, did well at it. Then, you know. He died young, unfortunately. Car accident. A car is a way of travelling—you know what, forget that, cars aren't important. His life was good."

"Yes?"

"Yes."

"And then he died?"

"Yes."

"And then what happened?"

Steven paused. "After my son died? What happened to him?"

"Yes."

Steven exhaled. "I don't know. Nobody really knows what happens after you die." He thought for a moment, then amended: "The people who run Humanity know. It's possible that everyone comes back here, just with their memories deleted."

They were quiet together for a moment. He listened to the breathing of his mother. Soothing. He wondered if Yesterday could hear hers; hard to tell what's in other people's heads. Hard to say.

"Steven?"

"Yes?"

"I think I'm gonna be born soon."

"Oh. Well. Best of luck. You'll do fine, I'm sure."

"Thank you." Yesterday seemed to be in a mist of violets and golds. He wondered if she'd be born into a bed of flowers. He wasn't sure, now, if that was a thing that happened for real or just in the fetus-dreams. Memory going.

"Hey, Steve? One more question before I have to go."

He braced himself. "Alright. Shoot."

"Is The Mother beautiful?"

Steve relaxed. Finally, an easy question. "Yes. Yes. All mothers are beautiful."

And though it wasn't much of an answer, it seemed enough for his friend. That evening, she was born in peace.

Steven Hall himself stayed in his mother's womb only a few months longer. By the end of his time, few fetuses alive remembered who he was, remembered the voice that disrupted their dream-song with such wildness that they shut him out forever. Only three fetuses observed his passing then: one who watched with pity, a second who watched with admiration.

The third fetus was barely an embryo when Steven disrupted the fetus-song to prophesy, and that fetus believed him with all his heart—believed in many mothers, believed in light from the sky, believed that a mother has arms. There wasn't much for the fetus to do with this belief, so he simply closed it up inside his belly and let it be.

And his life before birth was good.

Four.

Private Diary Bella Cholle, Director of Disaster

Notes: 08/09/2068

There's still so much we don't know about The Algorithm, even after decades of study. How does it account for weather potentials? What are the blue numbers on people's profiles tracking? Why does it purr on Halloween?

Who made it?

Did we make it? Somehow?

Unrelated: I received a Petition for Major Life Change form from Rainy Ellis today. Request for a body alteration. It's unorthodox, of course. She's young, younger than me. It'd be easy to reject.

But. That form is a hassle to fill out. It's ninety-seven pages long. Not how I'd choose to spend my time, but—Rainy Ellis. Perhaps it calls for an in-person interview.

Perhaps she's up for talking about it over coffee. It's a big life change, after all.

I'll bet there's a lot we could talk about.

Two Black Cats

by W.T. Paterson

It was a beautiful morning in May, and North Korea had once again threatened a nuclear strike. A crazed man had been arrested for cannibalism two towns away, and Joselyn Calloway was buried while her family wept, silently cursing Perry for talking their beautiful, successful, charming girl into marrying him.

Perry stood alone, dressed in a wrinkled black suit, unwashed and wild hair atop his head like a bird's nest, dark sunglasses across his eyes, and an unlit cigarette hanging from his dry lips. He could see Mrs. Calloway and Amanda staring him down with their thin, judgmental eyebrows. The worst part was that he probably agreed with what they were thinking. Their girl was too good for him, and they had no idea what she saw in Perry.

"I'm going to say something," Amanda said to Mrs. Calloway.

"Not here," the woman said and stiffened her back against the cool morning breeze. "Let the lawyers scare him first."

One by one, the family placed thornless roses on top of the cherry wood casket and rubbed their palms over the smooth lacquer. One by one, they whispered their goodbye as tears and mascara etched tributaries into their cheeks. One by one, they watched their beautiful girl lowered into her final resting place as pipers played a droning melody into the sunny May morning.

Perry dug through his pocket for the lighter, flamed the cigarette, and walked back to his ill-maintained sedan without once approaching the casket. As he left, he could feel the piercing gaze of the women trying to burn a hole into the back of his head.

"I know," he grumbled. "And it's working."

Perry was tall and slender, neither athletic nor scrawny. He was the type of guy who always seemed to be around but never had a specific purpose for being anywhere. He just…was. Always finding employment at low-wage, low-responsibility jobs like video rental shops or discount booze outlets, he never wanted much out of life. In return, life didn't give him much.

One time at The Liquor King, a group of women came in and complained about a drunken man out front attempting to grope customers. Perry looked outside and saw Charles, the local homeless guy with an untamed hair and frazzled beard, starting to play with himself through a hole in his dirty grey sweatpants.

"That guy?" he asked, pointing outside. The women nodded. "Okay, one sec."

Perry walked through the sliding glass doors as a burst of fresh air pushed against his face, put his foot against Charles's backside, and shoved him face first down the steps onto the newly paved parking lot.

"All set," he said, coming back inside, pulse barely raised above resting.

Among those women was Jocelyn, who was immediately taken.

"He's just so…raw," she said to her sister Amanda later that night. "He didn't care about what anyone else thought. Just, didn't care."

"He's a cashier at a liquor store?" Amanda asked skeptically.

"It was refreshing. No games, no BS, he just…was."

"Mom is going to flip."

"Isn't that kind of what I'm saying though?" she asked, wondering what it would be like to exist in a world without.

Joselyn was tall and angular with a sharp nose and chin and cheekbones, sharp hips, and even sharp knuckles. It was like she was equipped to slice her way through life. The only thing soft about her was the thick mane of brown hair pointing straight down at her shoulders.

When she went back to The Liquor King the next day to see if Perry was interested in getting a drink at a proper bar, the first thing Perry asked with his slow inward gaze was, "You buyin'?"

It never occurred to Perry that this proposition might lead to love, to a sense of fulfillment, to a better quality of life. Nor did he think it would lead to leukemia and aggressive treatments that quickly failed, which would shatter the life he had managed to find his way into.

And so he went out with Jocelyn, fell in love with her so madly that when she found out she was dying, two weeks after moving into her lakeside A frame, he pleaded with the powers that be to take him instead. Inside of a month, the powers did not acquiesce to his request.

*

"Isn't there someone you can stay with?" Amanda asked, standing in the foyer of the cabin. She looked like Joselyn, only meaner. Her voice echoed around the wooden room like a small rubber ball. Two black cats in blue collars poked their heads through the balustrade in curiosity. A television was mounted above the fireplace playing the local news on mute. A car crash on the interstate had slowed down traffic leaving the city. North

Korean relations had reached a standstill. A celebrity had visited a children's hospital in a superhero costume.

"Nope," Perry said, stalking between rooms looking for his fishing knife. His dark blue tee shirt was dirty and two sizes too large. His baggy tan cargo pants were as scuffed as his well-worn work boots.

"No family?" Amanda tried.

"Brother faked his own death when I was sixteen and is who-knows-where. Don't know my parents. So…no."

The cats were watching him pace from their mount. Amanda was aggressively rubbing her forehead.

"You do know what position this puts us all in, right?"

"I'll be fine," Perry said, opening a drawer and clanging through the contents. Rubber bands, a cooking mitt, spare buckshot for the rifle above the back door.

"She left you a lot, Per. Some of it, I don't know if it was hers to give. The lawyers have to go over it."

"Okay," he said, pulling out a butcher blade and looking at the sharpness. He ran it under his chin to see if it would peel off any hair. It did.

"The family is flying to England for two weeks to scatter the ashes. I won't be able to collect the cats until then. Can you handle that?"

"For two weeks? Yeah. Anything longer, though, and I eat the damn things," he said, pointing the knife at Amanda and then at the cats.

"You really should talk to the lawyers."

"They know where to find me," he said and then kicked open the back door with a fishing rod in hand, letting the screen slam shut behind with a high-pitched crack.

"These are indoor cats, Perry! Make sure they don't get out!" Amanda said, reaching up and giving the black cats some chin scratches. The cats purred like their lungs were mini engines. "I'll be back before you know it, babies."

*

It was nearing sundown when Perry returned to the kitchen with a recently caught monkfish. The cats anxiously watched from the doorway and rubbed the back of his ankles when he started to prep the catch.

Perry ran a knife along the scales as they started falling off like excess glitter from a birthday card. He hooked two fingers deep into the gills and, after slicing along the centerline, ripped the head and spine away from the meat in one fell swoop. It let out a wet crack and sent small pieces of entrails onto the countertop.

The cats began aggressively rubbing the back of Perry's legs and stretching their front paws up the side of his thigh.

"Get out of here!" he growled and shoved the cats backwards with his shin. "Y'all are hunters. If you're hungry, go hunt."

The two black cats sat off to the side, their tails flopping gently as though they were being filled and drained of air. They watched Perry with interest and curiosity, their gaze never breaking, attention never diverting.

Perry prepped a frying pan over the stove and lathered the bottom with a thin coating of olive oil. When it started to pop and boil, he put one of the freshly sliced hunks of meat into the pan and listened to it sizzle. The cats watched as he started cleaning up the remains. He saw them watching. They—who reminded him of Joselyn, of what it meant to love and lose, of the pain of surviving—stared back with equal confusion.

"I got nothin' for ya," he said, watching the meat start to change color in the pan. "We're on our own."

Anger welled up as he said it out loud. So did regret and longing and emptiness. His knees started to tremble, and so did something connecting his eyes and throat. One of the cats, the heavier of the two, jumped up to the counter next to the oven as Perry stared off into a memory. It sniffed the cooking meal, then Perry's elbow without the man noticing, and then it rubbed its head along his forearm with a soft purr.

Perry looked at the cat, startled.

"Get down from there," he said, shooing the cat away. "Unless you want to end up in the pan too." The cat leapt and scampered underneath a small table stacked with junk mail to sit with his brother. The two watched again as though providing play-by-play in a silent, secret language.

As he sat down to eat in front of the television and fireplace, the cats followed Perry to the couch and watched him sloppily eat from the opposite end. The television was still on mute. Birds chirped outside as the sun dipped behind the horizon, which allowed the world to dip into a land of shadows.

"Is that what it's like to die?" he asked out loud, watching as the details of a white birch faded into a dark silhouette. He placed his plate onto the soft cushion beside him, the place where Joselyn used to sit and talk to him about how humans were just one small piece of nature's vast puzzle.

"We're not as important as we think," she said, one night after receiving the terminal diagnosis. "Look outside. That'll be here long after we're gone."

"What's the point of anything existing after we're gone?" he tried.

"It's okay to be scared," she said as she took Perry's hand. He squeezed back gently, but couldn't meet her caring, hazel eyes. "I'm scared too."

It felt like a lifetime ago, but it wasn't. The house they shared for those few short months was forever haunted by Perry's memory of Joselyn. Every window, every corner, every piece of furniture reminded him of her, and there was no escape because there was nowhere else to go. The lawyers were actively trying to find ways to get him out of the cabin permanently, even though it was left to him. The problem was that the Calloway family had financed the land and the construction, and they owned the property. Although it was in Joselyn's name, lawyers were trying to argue that everything really belonged to the family. As such, they argued, Perry had no claim. At most, he had sixty days before it was brought before a judge.

If he lost, he couldn't afford an appeal, and so he had to rely on hope, which hadn't served him ever in his life before.

Snapping out of the daydream, he saw the two cats lick the dinner plate beside him clean and then look up with big, curious, loving eyes.

"I don't know how to do this," he whispered, and the smaller of the cats, the long slender one, sniffed Perry's fingers and licked the callused edges with a long, sandpaper tongue.

*

That night, he had horrible, painful dreams of Joselyn. They were standing at the edge of the lake like they had when she was living. In his dream, he could still smell her.

"I'm no good. I'm rotten," he said.

"It must be weird then," Joselyn said, her voice moving like soft wind across the surface of the lake. "To have someone love you when you don't love yourself."

"I'm full of holes."

"Aren't we all?"

His dream played the scene of his brother faking his death. The burned and charred corpse of a year-old brown bear. The police questioning him for hours. The feeling that he was only worth a person's time if they could get something from him.

"Can't you be like my brother? Can't I imagine you still alive out there and one day maybe you'll return?" he asked. Lake water began to rise at their feet, first swallowing their ankles and then inching up to their knees.

"That would be worse," Joselyn said. "It would be a thousand times worse."

"Remember our first night together? Those damn cats kept jumping on the bed, and we had to shoo them away. You laughed, and I kept getting angry and threatening to carve them up into burgers. But then I got so angry that I started laughing, and we laughed, and there was nothing in the world that had ever made me feel so good."

"The thing about holes is that when they're filled with something real—something human—we start to see ourselves as fully human."

"Why me?" he asked. The water was past their waist and rising quickly to their necks. In the dream, he knew that the rising water was all of the tears he could never cry.

"Because you're you and no one else."

As the water reached her neck, Perry watched as her eyes became sunken inside of her skull. He watched the hair thin on her head. She coughed in deep, phlegm-filled bursts like she would after treatments. When the water reached her eyes, he watched as Joselyn stopped struggling and gave herself to death as a welcome reprieve.

He shot awake, gasping for breath and sweating wildly.

Both cats were in bed with him. It was the first time since Joselyn had been gone that they'd slept on the bed. The heavier cat was on his chest, tucked into a perfect black ball, purring loudly. The vibrations of the purrs were right above his heart, and as he gulped down air, he felt how soothing the sound was. The longer, more slender cat was stretched against his hip and legs in a superman pose as if to say I'm here for you. They both woke and looked at Perry with sleepy, slow eyes. The slender one yawned, stood up, and sniffed Perry's eyebrow, and then curled himself into the crook of Perry's arm.

"Y'all have bad dreams too?" he asked. He ran his palm across their soft heads, and the light affection made the cats lean into him with delight. "What are your names? Something Greek, like Thor and Apollo, I think? That's no good. I'll call you Grim," he said to the heavier cat. "And I'll call you Reaper," he said to the slender cat, giving them both chin scratches. "Just don't expect me to keep giving you stuff. Amanda the Antagonist will be back for you soon."

And even that thought began to pull at his heart.

*

Perry walked barefoot through the pressed dirt and clay roads to the general store. The lack of good sleep made his body feel three times as heavy, and his stomach growled like a feral bobcat. The fish hadn't been biting as much as they once did.

His cell phone buzzed with yet another voicemail. That made five he hadn't listened to. Perry dug the phone out of his pocket, tapped into the voicemail, and put everything on speakerphone.

Mr. Andrews, this is Attorney Robert Baumgart calling on behalf of the Calloway fami… delete.

Hi again, this is Robert Baumgart. Not sure if you received my last message, but… delete.

Mr. Andrews, this is silly. If you don't talk to us, the consequences could be quite… delete.

Listen, you rat, Mrs. Calloway's voice alarmingly shrill, be a man and do something with your life. Get out of ours. I made some calls to people I know and gave them your info, so… delete.

Hello, this message is for Perry Andrews. My name is Monica Green, and I am following up on your inquiry about enlisting in the Marines. If you… delete.

That last one gave him slight pause. He wasn't sure if, in blind mourning, he had considered the military an option or if Mrs. Calloway was trying to manipulate him.

As he pushed open the door to the general store, he tucked the phone back into his pocket.

"Man, you see this?" the owner, an unusually large man named Frank Albatross, said, pointing to a box TV near the counter. "Logistics truckers on strike. Somethin' to do with the military shutting down routes? Must be why I ain't got an order in two weeks."

"Wow," Perry said, unimpressed. He walked down the shoulder-height aisles grabbing bread, peanut butter, some chips, and a bag of beef jerky. The selection was noticeably slimming down.

"I wonder if it's all hokey-pokey, ya know? Maybe North Korea ain't even a threat, and it's all a way to keep us inside and scared. Hell, maybe the Earth is actually flat, and lizard people control us all."

"Lizard people," Perry echoed without any affectation. He brought his haul to the counter and plopped it down.

"You got cash? Card machine ain't workin' right."

"How about I pay you later?"

"Nice try, amigo. Ain't the 1950s no more."

Perry cursed and picked the food up to put it back on the shelves. Frank went back to watching the TV. When Frank wasn't looking, Perry pocketed the bag of beef jerky and, on a whim, a whole stack of canned cat food.

"Fish aren't biting like they used to," he said, slowly strolling the aisles, waiting for his moment to exit, hoping Frank wouldn't notice the bulges by his hips.

"You talkin' 'bout the pond?"

"Yup."

"You askin' why there ain't no fish biting in a pond where you been fishin' the last few months? I dunno, son, maybe it's because it's a pond that you been fishin' the last few months."

"Great. Awesome," Perry said. Frank went back to watching the television.

"And now they tryin' to sell me life insurance! Ain't that a crock? Life insurance. Ain't no such thing." Frank shook his head slowly without breaking away from the screen.

"Okay," Perry said. He quietly left the store without the owner even acknowledging it.

*

Perry came home to find his front door wide open and the aluminum screen door ajar. There was a brief moment of panic where he thought that maybe one of the lawyers was inside and waiting, but he also seemed to remember that he hadn't bothered to close it when he left for the store.

He shouldered his way inside and tossed the jerky onto the table next to the junk mail. He placed the cat food cans onto the counter next to the stove and whistled for the cats. He wondered if they responded to whistles like dogs, and then he remembered how Joselyn would make kissy noises to get their attention. He tried, and then made clicking sounds with the tongue on the roof of his mouth. Nothing. Perry looked around the corner, then into the sitting room. Finally, by the back slider, he saw Grim staring outside with fur completely fluffed like he had been startled.

"What's your deal?" he said, and then he looked onto the back patio to see Reaper outside slowly backing into the side of the house with fur also fluffed. A bobcat three times his size was slowly stalking forward. Grim was growling in haunting low gutturals, unable to go help his brother. Reaper quickly caught eyes with Perry, and Perry immediately recognized the fear in the small cat. It had never been outside, had never known the dangers, and now found itself up against a literal wall.

Perry knew he had one shot, and it had to be fast. Throw open the slider and charge the bobcat. It would either sprint toward Reaper, snatch him up, and take off into the woods, or it would simply run off to save itself. He hoped it was the latter, so he threw open the door. The adrenaline made him feel powerful. Grim ran out beside him to his brother and posted up.

"Three on one! What's up?!" Perry yelled, soccer kicking the air. Stunned, the bobcat turned and sprinted back into the forest, narrowly missing a shot to the face from Perry's bare foot. He followed the large cat for a few steps before turning around as the two house cats ran back inside. Reaper had something in his mouth. Perry checked one more time to make sure the bobcat wasn't lurking and didn't see anything, so he went inside and closed the slider.

"What was that all about?"

He saw the two cats hunched over a dead bird. Reaper looked up proud and let out a soft mew.

"Well, look at you, little hunter," Perry said, impressed. "Can't say I know how to prep a bird, but my guess is that nature gave you the knowledge." He let them be while he pulled the spare buckshot out of the drawer, loaded it into the rifle that was hanging above the door, and went out to shoot the bobcat in the face if it tried to sneak back. This time, he made sure to fully close the door behind him.

*

Perry stood guard from the afternoon until dusk, but the bobcat wasn't coming back. It just wasn't.

Just as he was about to head inside, a black Mercedes Benz pulled up on the dirt-and-clay driveway. A man in a pressed pinstripe suit got out with slicked-back hair and a shiny, gold watch.

"Perry Andrews? My name is Robert Baumgart and…"

Perry cocked the gun.

"Okay, it's a bad time. I'll come back later," the lawyer said, putting his hands in the air and slowly retreating to his car. He pulled away and sped off, kicking up a trail of red dust behind.

When Perry went back inside, his stomach screaming, he saw the bird had been eaten. The bones had been picked clean of meat, the inedible entrails shucked aside, and small piles of sick were near the oven with slick, wet pieces of feathers. The cats were asleep next to each other on the couch looking as happy as he'd ever seen them. Watching them sleep made him feel some sort of peace, even if he couldn't articulate exactly why.

Before he turned in for the night, he popped open a can of wet food and left it on the ground for the cats, because, if even for the night, he didn't want them to have to hunt to stay alive.

*

Perry awoke with the cats beside him again. They were both alert and looking at the window nervously.

"Is he back? The bobcat?!" Perry said, sitting up and looking outside. He was ready to go out and inflict a healthy portion of street justice, but something else grabbed his attention. The window was open, but the outside world wasn't making any sound. No birds chirping, no distant rumble of airplanes, not even the wind pushing through dry forest leaves. The cats weren't purring, and they trotted back and forth on the edge of the bed, acting skittish.

He pulled out his phone and started seeing all of the notifications and emails.

North Korea had attacked. They bombed a number of major cities with nuclear weapons. The death toll was catastrophic, and the residual damage was horrifying. Fast-spreading radiation. Guerilla mercenaries staging coups. Martial law enacted. All planes grounded, all transportation halted.

A video of an analyst detailed exactly how the U.S. had failed to prevent the invasion.

"We naively trained and funded a number of sleeper cells already inside of our borders. Now, we forever pay the price of our own ignorance. Goodbye, free speech. Goodbye, free trade. Goodbye to every luxury that we have taken for granted."

There were other video uploads of wild riots and looting. People sobbed in the streets. Drone footage of decimated cities and suburbs.

Perry shot out of bed and ran to the front door. He grabbed the rifle and tried to do a quick inventory of the food left in the kitchen: a bag of half-eaten beef jerky, some lentil soup stored in the cupboard, and a few cans of cat food. Not nearly enough to sustain. If he could loot the convenience store, it might be able to buy him some time before...before what? He wondered how quickly the radiation would spread, how fast the survivors would take to the woods, how quickly the human race would turn on itself, devouring the country from the inside out. He looked at the gun and saw only that he could fire two, maybe three times total before the ammo ran out. Were there even animals left to hunt? Did enough people still know how? How long until those animals ran out?

Panic began to set in, and Perry decided to run toward the convenience store. Barefoot, he clomped down the dirt-and-clay roads, making it halfway before getting paranoid that someone might walk into the cabin and loot the little he had left; so instead, he turned around and ran home, leaving bloody footprints on the small rocks pressed into the road.

Posted up inside the cabin, he fixed the gun on the entryway and waited for a reason to pull the trigger. Survival became the only option.

Hunger set in.

The beef jerky ran out by nightfall.

The next day, Perry tried to fish but caught nothing. The day after was also a bust. The cats were the only ones being fed. The lentil soup was hardly sustaining. He hadn't seen another form of life for half a week.

Then, on the fifth day, birds started chirping. Though, he wasn't sure if they were actually making noise or if hunger was playing a murderous trick on his brain.

Sitting by the door fingering the trigger of the gun, Perry watched the cats bathe themselves, their pink tongues lapping the black fur of their little bodies. Their meaty legs, their soft underbellies, their floppy tails. Joselyn used to sit and watch the cats for hours. It brought her so much happiness.

"They just know what to do," she said. Her voice was clear in his memories. "Nature supports nature."

And that's when he got the idea, his best shot at survival.

The cats.

He could eat them.

Perry took a quick inventory. He had the knives to prep them, the stove was still working the last time he checked. Indoor cats, Amanda had called them, so they would never be far out of his reach. Each one could provide enough meat to last a few days. Those few days might create enough of a window to figure out how to get to the next step.

Stay alive, his mind played on repeat over, and over, and over.

The cats jumped off the couch and rubbed the back of Perry's legs before pawing each other in the face and wrestling in the middle of the living room floor as though the collapse of modern civilization wasn't happening. It wasn't like he was attached to the damn things. It wasn't like they were his cats.

The more Perry thought about it, the more the option became real. They'd already helped him begin to heal after Joselyn died, so why not use them as a catalyst to finish the journey? Nature supports nature. It would be quick and painless, the flash of a knife under their soft chins. He looked at the rifle. Maybe it would be faster. If anything, it was an advantage to have the cats living under his watchful eye.

He tracked them for the rest of the day as he pondered, played out scenarios, and grew dangerously hungry. They saved him once before, and he knew they could do it again.

By nightfall, he opened the final can of wet food and placed it on the floor of the living room near the fireplace. Grim and Reaper trotted in, attacking the final portion with wet, smacking bites.

"The two of you showed me kindness when you had no reason to," he said aloud, holding the rifle with shaky hands and arms. "Like Joselyn, you took a chance on me. Now she's gone. Most anyone I've ever known is gone. I've never been more alone and…"

He stopped. As he was speaking, he realized that there was another way out.

"Why should it be me that survives? How vain to think that this world should support me. Who am I without those that loved me?"

He cocked the gun. The two cats leapt away from the plate startled and looked up at Perry tucking the gun under his chin and sliding a big toe near the trigger.

"Nature supports nature. Why should I eat you when you could eat me? I can give myself to you, the only two who were ever there for me, and you would survive. Joselyn is right. Nature will survive long after we will, and I don't want to live in a world without her and without you."

The cats looked panicked, ready to dart away. They tilted their heads with pointy ears to try and look at Perry, who was now sobbing uncontrollably. It was like they knew they were about to say goodbye.

"And so it goes," Perry said, stepping on the trigger, hearing a brief but loud crack, and having the world suddenly go dark like a fast-setting sun turning trees into silhouettes. The cats furiously scattered.

By nightfall, they curled up by his lifeless feet, knowing exactly what it was they had to do come morning.

Skylar Is Not Sitting on His Bed Somewhere

by Vivian McInerny

When the first car hit, it landed harmlessly in a cornfield in the middle of nowhere. A farmer harvesting an adjacent field saw a flash of light, heard a kaboom, and discovered the Toyota Camry standing nose first amid the still, green stalks of corn. The front of the car was crumpled and buried halfway up the doors in dirt from the impact.

"I'll be damned," the farmer said aloud, or at least that's what he said he said when he recalled the story for the local radio station. "I seen a lot of things in my time, but this is a first."

He had no idea how the car ended up in his cornfield but happily provided three theories: 1) College kids on a nearby campus pulled a prank.

2) A cargo plane of Toyotas had a defective hatch latch. 3) A UFO tried to abduct the car, but the vehicle proved too heavy.

The dean of the small Christian college assured the public that his students had done no such thing, and he praised God for sparing them. The car manufacturer said its vehicles were assembled in factories in Mexico and transported by land, never air, to the USA. It should be noted that not a single alien came forward to deny the UFO shenanigans.

Television news had a field day, literally. They all sent camera crews to Podunk, Podunkistan, to get footage of the smashed car while earnest affiliates, hoping this was their big break to the networks, pointed out the obvious: A car fell from the sky. A business reporter from the Wall Street Journal, noting the lack of identifying license plates on the car, suggested its serial number might provide clues to its origin. Everyone relaxed knowing a federal investigation would solve the mystery and the culprits would be caught and punished.

Facebook was full of silly memes about suicidal jumper cars, rideshares gone awry, and farmers harvesting fields full of vehicles. By the weekend, SNL had a skit about Putin dropping a car on Alec Baldwin as the president, all while a soothing voiceover by Matthew McConaughey oozed about luxury leather seats and horsepower. Honestly, it was funnier than it sounds.

Investigators gathered information on all cars reported stolen or missing. They said the serial number on the wreck wasn't legible and, so, drew no conclusions. For weeks afterward, pundits opined on the cause of the falling car until the public's interest also started falling and they moved onto other topics. And then, out of nowhere, a second car dropped from the sky and killed a man in Los Angeles.

This time, several people witnessed the fall. It was a Saturday afternoon, and they were doing ordinary Saturday things: shooting hoops, working on their cars, drinking on the front stoop with friends—when there was a flash-and-kaboom.

"I thought it was the cops, one of those stun grenades," said a guy. "But then I look again and see J.J.'s gone. I mean, he is gone!"

Poor J.J. was minding his own business selling cans of Coke in the neighborhood, an entrepreneur of sorts. He was a familiar sight, pulling around an old cooler mounted to a skateboard, a red-and-white plastic thing filled with ice and cans of soda. Some said he bought the soft drinks in bulk at the big box store and sold them individually for a profit. Others said the cases fell off the backs of delivery trucks.

"He was a good man," said a woman, raising a can of Mountain Dew in a kind of memorial toast. "A good man just trying to do right by his family. His sodas were good too. Ice cold, always."

Her current soft drink was evidently of a less-than-ideal temperature.

"He was fair and square, J.J.," said a guy with a dog. "He never marked things up greedy-high, you know what I'm saying? RIP, J.J."

The owner of the only convenience store within miles admitted he had called the cops on the unlicensed soda-seller in the past.

"I was sick and tired of dealing with return deposits on cans I didn't sell. I just wanted him to stop," he said. "But J.J. didn't deserve this. No one deserves this."

By "this," he meant a car falling from the sky to squish him like a bug. Everybody agreed that such a harsh punishment for selling sodas, stolen or not, was not warranted.

All the television news anchors solemnly announced the tragedy "too graphic" to show viewers, as though they were taking the moral high ground, when, in fact, they were forbidden by the FCC to air anything so gruesome. However, regulations didn't stop them from running endless loops of a moody shot of yellow, plastic, caution tape flapping in the breeze around an area still sticky with soda.

A GIF of a Coke can rolling through deserted urban streets like aluminum tumbleweed accompanied by sad, penny-whistle music trended on Twitter and Instagram.

@PopGirl91 wrote: This gets me every time. Sad face emoji.

@TiasMom: I know, right?

@TheJackster: It's an **cking commercial, you morons!

The thread quickly devolved into a remarkably ill-informed argument about algorithms, guerrilla marketing, and how only fools gave away personal information taking online surveys to determine which Friend/Kardashian/Harry Potter character they were. Someone suggested both falling cars were part of a stealth marketing plan by Toyota. But then the second car turned out to be a Subaru.

Once again, investigators couldn't identify the serial numbers.

People said they'd never buy a Toyota or Subaru again and called for a nationwide boycott. On YouTube, a guy livestreamed setting fire to an old model Legacy in his driveway. Commentators said the twenty-five-year-old piece of junk wasn't worth the gasoline and matches it took to ignite it. When the fire leapt to the guy's garage, he stopped videoing; but by then, his neighbors had their cell phones out and so captured the heroics of the firefighters from multiple angles.

About three weeks later, it happened again. This time, a Chevy. It landed on a public high school in Colorado, crashed right through the roof of the cafeteria. Miraculously, only two kids were killed. It could have been much worse, but it happened in the late afternoon when most students had already gone home. The flattened boys, both freshman, were holding their first gamers club meeting, and, fortunately and unfortunately, no one showed up. The next day, though, hundreds of teary-eyed students gathered near the wreckage to place teddy bears, flowers, and an old-school Game Boy on the rubble while television crews offered condolences and asked students if they had any personal stories to share. A pretty blonde named Mariah-something said that the one boy sat next to her in science, and they might have been assigned lab partners if he hadn't died. And then she started crying again.

The next night on the Famous Seamus Show, the host said an astute viewer noticed that “two suspicious-looking characters” in the background of the Colorado school video looked very similar to guys in the background of the earlier Los Angeles video. Famous Seamus ran a split screen of both clips, stopped the tapes, blew them up, and digitally enhanced two dark figures. One appeared to have a beard, or maybe a five o’clock shadow, or maybe just a shadow-shadow.

“No one is accusing them of anything,” said Famous Seamus, sounding reasonable enough. “I’m just saying that if they are indeed innocent bystanders, why don’t they come forward and identify themselves?”

He paused. The camera zoomed in. He looked directly into the lens, his eyes a startling shade of blue.

“Please, we beg of you,” he said. “Just identify yourselves.”

For several days after, social media blew up with sightings—from Charlottesville, Virginia, to Orange County, California—of the falling car terrorists or crisis actors or whatever they were. I seen someone that looks just like the bearded guy coming out of a mosk in Kansas City. Someone demanded to know why the police didn’t arrest him. KCKPD is too PC and their going to get us all killed! Someone wanted to know what all the alphabets stood for. Kansas City Kansas Police Department, dumbass, came the response. Another tweet said: It happened in Missouri! There's two KC, double dumbass! Others jumped in with their stories about corruption due to fascists, corruption due to anti-fascists, stupid laws that handcuffed the police from doing their jobs, and other laws that gave the police too much power.

The president invited the families of the two dead boys to the White House. It had to be postponed after a kerfuffle when the president tweeted, They’ll probably blame Russia!! Turned out, the grandmother of one of the kids was born in Russia and missed the subtlety of the president’s “they” jab. The press secretary announced that it was clear the president was joking and that the mainstream media was trying, once again, to divide this country. The visit was rescheduled for the following week. The other kid's parents were divorced and remarried, and so there was some back-and-forth about who was and wasn't invited to the White House. In the end, all three parental couples, two grandparents, four full-siblings, two half-siblings, and a baby not related by blood to either boy but carried in for posterity wore their Sunday best and stood in a carefully orchestrated cluster while the president shook hands and patted shoulders.

"This guy voted for me, didn't you," said the president, squeezing a dad's hand and slapping his back. "Good guy. Great people, Colorado. Great people."

The president then took a seat at his desk to sign a bill to form a special task force to look into the cause of the falling cars while the miscellaneous relatives—half, full, and step—stood peering over his shoulder as he formed the big, loopy letters of his signature like it was really something to see. The baby showed no interest. The president turned the signed bill toward the cameras to show everyone his fine work, then held the pen over his right shoulder, offering it as a souvenir. When two dads made a grab for it, the president laughed good-naturedly and addressed someone off camera.

"Everyone wants the pen. Can you blame them? Get them both pens, will you? Get them all pens, every one of them! We can do that, right? I'm asking her, and I'm the president," he said in a self-deprecating way, and everyone laughed and everyone got a souvenir pen.

The next day, a fourth car fell on the Interstate 90 outside Chicago during rush hour. The media immediately dubbed the incident "Crush Hour." The car killed two people directly when it flattened a rideshare Honda and three more people indirectly after they swerved to avoid the crash and instead jumped the concrete guard rail into oncoming traffic. The total number of injuries was seven. While panels of experts discussed the ramifications on several talk shows, news of the fifth and sixth cars broke.

A Ford landed in rural Georgia, another near the northern border of Arizona. Amazingly, no one was hurt, but people were still shook. Nowhere felt safe. And then it was discovered that yet another car, a Cadillac, had fallen around the same time in South Dakota, killing a buffalo. It was one of those domesticated bison raised for meat and destined to the slaughterhouse anyway, but still. It seemed like some sort of omen, a symbol of the American West squashed to a hamburger patty. A national TV weatherman started mapping what he dubbed "car strikes," like lightning strikes. The term stuck. Pretty soon all the local weather forecasters did their own versions of the same.

Then it leaked that not a single one of the seven falling cars had a serial number. It wasn't that the vehicles were so badly damaged that investigators couldn't read the numbers. Serial numbers had never been issued. Suffice to say that intrigue and public fear ramped up.

People demanded to know why cars fell only on American soil. Some argued it was because our great nation was also of great size and therefore presented a bigger target. But other countries—specifically Russia, India, and China, not to mention the entire continent of Africa—were also massive, yet reported no strikes. Some people suspected those governments quashed any reports to avoid panicking the masses. In fact, no other country in the entire world had experienced a single strike. It had to be something specific about the United States.

If falling cars were part of a foreign operative plan to sow panic, it was working. The Department of Defense proposed shooting down not only the cars but also any and all space junk, including satellites, NASA debris, and floating bits and pieces from abandoned international space stations. People flipped out. They thought the government was going to take out their mobile phone and satellite televisions to leave them helpless. The words Uncle Sam Wants You in the Dark Ages with an updated image of the vintage pointy-finger recruitment poster were spray painted on walls and bridges nationwide and attributed to Banksy. Banksy denied it. A high-ranking retired general and regular news show panelist said that shooting down all space debris would also serve to demonstrate to our enemies "both perceived and unknown" our prowess as a reigning super power.

"But, Sir," said the host. "Wouldn't those shot pieces also fall to Earth, further endangering American lives?"

"We would do our best to intercept objects over the Atlantic or Pacific where they most likely would cause no harm," he said.

"But there are no guarantees," the host pushed.

"Look," said the General. "One way or another, that stuff is coming for us. And you better believe..."

Suddenly: Flash! Kaboom! And just like that, the general, the host, and two other panelists were taken out by a black SUV on live television.

To call what followed in the coming days pandemonium is an understatement. The DOW tanked. Ammunition sales soared. Schools closed for the summer, though it was only April. People stockpiled food, and when stores ran low on inventory, the looting started. There were riots, blackouts, and walkouts. Several high-powered CEOs stepped down from their positions, foregoing lucrative incentives to remain at the helm, claiming they wanted to spend more time with their families. And they meant it. International airports were mob scenes as people tried to bribe their way onto sold-out flights, begging anywhere but here. Cars lined up for days at both the Canadian and Mexican borders. The Department of State issued a temporary moratorium on passports, citing a backlog of applicants, but everyone knew it was the government's desperate attempt to stop the mass exodus of citizens and assure those remaining that they were, if not safe, at least not alone.

It was nice to have Mom around more. Declared a non-essential employee in the shutdown, she seemed relieved to have the decision made for her. My big brother moved back home. I thought he'd be annoying, but he'd changed. He dug out an old World of Warcraft CD and let me play. The neighbors started pooling food in backyard potlucks. If anyone was saving a bottle of wine for a special occasion, they decided now was the time to pop the cork. They poured for anyone over thirteen who asked. I tasted my first champagne. Oh, and for the record, I don't weigh four hundred pounds, and I'm not sitting on my bed somewhere, okay? I'm right here. And all I need is this laptop and the motivation.

Featherweight

by J. Castle

I woke up, and I knew it was going to be a shitty day, but I didn't really know why or to what extent. I just had that feeling, like, man, today is just going to be a day I wish I didn't wake up. I didn't realize it was going to end with me dead on the front bumper of a red Chevy Tahoe. Or really, I wouldn't have woken up at all. May as well die in your own bed if you're going to die anyway. Right?

It was near the end of October, and the weather was very strange. In fact, the whole summer it had been strange, so I wasn't really sure what that meant for the winter for me. It was at around this time that I usually got that familiar urge to start to head down south again. It was one of those things that I couldn't explain, but just happened, always around the same time. This year, though, it sort of felt like that on and off for the past few months. Because of the screwy weather.

On this day, it was overcast, and it had been for the past week or so. In fact, there was a good amount of rain earlier in the week, and it had really fucked with my nest. The good news, of course, was that there were tons of worms out. Relatively speaking. But, that really doesn't mean a damned thing when your house is waterlogged and sticky and smelly. All the amount of food in the world doesn't compare to a nice, clean bed. Really. Ask yourself the same question, and I think you'll agree. Even if you're a glutton.

I can't stand gluttons. I hope you're not one.

Saturdays are usually all right for me. There's a farmers market near the tree where I live, and I can wander around there and usually pick up some decent scraps and leftovers around closing time. This Saturday, I figured it would be something similar. It wasn't.

I don't, or I didn't, before I died, have a lady of my own. Truth is, I used to be mated to someone, but she left me for another guy. She didn't offer any explanation, really, but I knew what the reason was. I was a lousy lay. There. I said it. I was bad at the one thing I was supposed to be good at. It was disappointingly true. We both knew it, and we never talked about it. It's the kind of thing that just tears apart a relationship, and worse yet, it snowballs and grows and grows and grows until you can't even think about bringing it up. It's too huge at that point. Too colossal. Too personal.

She left me and never looked back. And while she never saw me again, I saw her pretty often. I never had a problem with her as a person, so naturally when she left, I had a lot of questions and unresolved issues I was dealing with. So it was also natural that I would seek her out and find her new nest. And would watch her from another tree. Right? What's unnatural about that? Just because there are stalking laws on the books doesn't mean that it isn't natural. I mean, they make lots of laws and rules to stop you from doing things that are fully natural. Otherwise, why would they need to make a law or rule about something? You just wouldn't do it if it was unnatural. Naturally.

She had been gone for about two weeks, which is a long time for my people, when I finally found her and started watching her from another tree. She was getting all cozy in her new nest with her new man. Truthfully, I couldn't blame her for what she was doing. I knew I was the reason for her leaving, and I knew that there wasn't anything I could do to change it. I had been to a therapist to try to understand if my sexual apprehension was a result of some innate mental deficiencies that I had not yet acknowledged. I had gone to a doctor to see if the problem was physical. My initial attempts at getting well did not help, and I became frustrated with the whole process and gave up. That was my fault. I really should have tried harder.

Anyways, I would watch her in her nest for a few hours a day sometimes. Objectively, yeah, it was probably pretty weird. But I couldn't help it. I needed to watch her. It gave me comfort. That is, until her man spotted me watching them one day. It was really awkward. All I need to tell you is that he looked right at me, we locked eyes, and I flew away. I know he knew not only that I was staring, but he also knew who I was. I'm sure she had told him all about me. Or at least I'd like to think she did. Either way, he looked at me so knowingly, there had to be some recognition there. I had to get the hell out of there, so I did.

The weather and its recent screwiness was starting to make me anxious. I really wanted to start my trip down south, and not being able to know if and when I could or should was really frustrating. I didn't want anything to do with my nest, my old life, and everything around me. Now, granted, there's no reason I couldn't just head south on my own accord if I really wanted to. But, that's just not how my people roll. You know? We don't go off of logic. We follow our guts. Intuition. Biology. All of that shit.

Well, all of that shit is probably what got me killed. Or at least I like to think that's what happened. It's too hard to face the reality that you are responsible for all of your actions and therefore the conditions that lead to your eventual and undeniable demise. That's why we believe in other things, like gods and mental conditions and oppression and the very real circumstances that hold us down, make us something else, decide our lives for us. Fate us to our fates. The truth is, that's all bullshit. We all know it, but we all lie to ourselves and everyone around us to make ourselves feel better. It's so stupid. But it's true.

So, despite me knowing better, I decided to stick around my current life and times and wait until biology and the weather told me it was time to move on. All right.

I woke up, and I knew it was going to be a shitty day, but I didn't really know why or to what extent. I just had that feeling, like, man, today is just going to be a day I wish I didn't wake up. The farmers market had been going on for an hour or two, which means I had been awake for maybe three or four hours. It was such a typical day, I didn't even need to think or act. It was all muscle memory. I would fly down from my nest and wander over to the market to see if any of the gluttons had dropped their samples on the ground. Unable to bend down, for that would resemble a stretch, which would resemble exercise, the gluttons would often leave their dropped samples where they lay. Which meant they were free for me to scoop up and fly back home with.

Dropped fruit samples are so much better than a worm. Trust me. I know that I'm supposed to like worms, but come on. They're worms. They're disgusting. Just because I can eat them doesn't mean that I want to.

I had picked up a few pieces of fruit before heading back to my nest. I still had that weird feeling that the day was going to be awful, and I remember thinking that very clearly as I approached my tree again. When I hopped up the branches and got nearer to my nest, that's when it hit me.

Not a feeling. Not a thought. Not a revelation. A literal hit. I got hit in the face with a shovel. Right in the fucking face! Now, before you start to overanalyze this, keep in mind that you're reading a story written by a dead bird. Suspend your disbelief for a few moments to realize that if that is possible, it is entirely possible that a shovel could hit me in the face while I'm up in a tree. Okay?

The feeling of the shovel was unlike anything I had ever felt against my beak. The cold metal was extremely flat—flatter than I'd have imagined if I had ever taken the time to imagine what it'd feel like if I was to get clocked in the face with a shovel. It was hard, unforgiving even, and it had a certain rusty smell that made me nauseous. Or, would have made me nauseous if I had time to comprehend what was happening. I have a few fleeting memories before I fell:

1. My feet were a lot less able to grip onto the branch than I would have expected. I always assumed that my grip was unfailingly strong. It is not. When faced with a shovel, literally, you lose a bit of the control of your extremities that you always assumed you had.
2. Weightlessness is a cool feeling when you're not in extreme pain. Weightlessness is not a cool feeling when you are in extreme pain. Keep that in mind.
3. My split-second gut instinct suggested that my old lady's new man was the shovel swinger.
4. I saw her face as I was falling, and I knew that my gut was wrong.
5. Again.

I hit the hood of the SUV first and then slowly rolled down toward the front until my body careened somewhat gracefully over the edge and onto the bumper, where I landed on my back and faced straight up at my nest, some fifteen feet away. I remember seeing a leaf fall down from the tree, and it ignited a feeling in me that made me think it might be time to head south soon. It made me sad and happy at the same time. I liked it when the leaves would fall. I liked new things. I liked moving.

I woke up, and I knew it was going to be a shitty day. I didn't realize it was going to end with me dead on the front bumper of a red Chevy Tahoe. The last moments of my life, I swelled with unavoidable regret. I feel like that probably happens to most people—and certainly most birds. But probably most people too. The truth is, we live our lives within the guidelines we're told to. We don't act out often because that would be wrong. We don't do much of anything, relatively speaking, because we're afraid of what might happen.

I realized on that shitty Saturday that what might happen if we did all of the things we wanted to do is no scarier than what might and will happen if we don't. In fact, there was one certainty of that day, and it was that in my final moments, I would be reminiscing on all of my memories, all of my decisions that had gotten me to where I was...all of my life, really. It didn't flash before my eyes because, really, there's too much in a life for it to go by so quickly.

The sad irony is that it all does go by too quickly. One moment you're eating fruit at the farmers market. The next, you're dead on the bumper of a red Chevy Tahoe. Fuck. I wish I had done more with myself.

I wish I had followed through with those doctor visits and appointments. I wish I had been a better man to my lady. I wish I had done all of the things I wanted to do, that I thought I should do. Like go down south earlier. Or poop on the gluttons at the farmers market. Or just sleep in that day and never leave my nest. Whatever it was, I wish I just did more of what I wanted to do and less of what I was supposed to do. I was, after all, a bird. Why did I spend so much time worrying about what other people think of me?

No matter. This is how it ended for me, that shitty Saturday. As I lay there, staring up at my old home and my old life, I knew that what had happened was meant to happen. Or at least I told myself that, to feel better. My eyes were getting heavy, and I knew I didn't have much time left, so I closed them and dreamed about winning the lottery.

The Sky Is Falling

by Emily Anne Griffin

It was shocking, at first. When Mayweather Smithie, the first of them, was found crushed under a pile of odds and ends, a garbage sack of unreasonably miscellaneous items—like a junk drawer but bigger—the whole town stood collectively agape. It clearly came from the sky, but no one could recall seeing an airplane that day. But really, no one ever paid that kind of attention. There was never anything to pay attention to in Timecapsule.

That is, not until the bodies started piling up. All the way up to the seventh victim: my pa, Danforth McWallswart.

Though, there's some debate about whether or not Pa is an actual victim, but I'll come back to that. I was talking about Mayweather here.

It was the third of July, and Mayweather was jaywalking across the street on her way back to the Holy Church of Our Almighty Independence Day float-decorating colloquium. She was carrying a box of red, white, and blue crepe paper, a bunch of oversized popsicle sticks, and an assortment of rhinestones. The bedazzled-cross assembly line ran short on materials, and Mayweather had trotted off righteously as Patience Hollyhocks apologized yet again. "The only way to get things done right around here is to have me do it," Mayweather said to the swinging door.

Anyway, Mayweather was on her way back to the church with her box, like I said, jaywalking...when out of nowhere, a Hefty bag took her out, right there in the middle of Main Street. If you'd never heard a car accident, you might have thought that's what made that noise, but as Jefferson Jeffries walked out of his Big Jay Hardware and Craft Shoppe, he didn't immediately see the wreckage. It wasn't until Patience came around the corner and saw that glistening trickle of blood pave a crack in the street, triggering in her the most guttural, carnal scream ever heard in Timecapsule, Tennessee, did Mr. Jeffries see the mess of hair and trash and paisley print. He rushed to her side as Miss Hollyhocks continued screaming and pointing from the sidewalk. From first sight, it was clear there was no saving her, so Mr. Jeffries began his examination of the scene. He stood, arms crossed looking over it all until there was nothing left to do but open the trash bag. From it, he pulled a length of plastic tubing, a kitchen sprayer, several partial bottles of Ajax, an empty bottle of dawn dish soap, a plunger, several assorted knobs, a faucet, and what appeared to have caused the fatal blow: a badly damaged garbage disposal.

"My God! It's everything but the kitchen sink."

Nobody knew what to make of it. But they sure talked about it.

"Never seen nothing like it."

"It was a freak accident."

Some said space aliens.

Laverne Bouffant, owner of Bouffant's Beehives and Buzzcuts, began running her mouth on some theory. Clearly, the good Lord was punishing Mayweather. "Maybe she ought to have minded her own mess rather than always harping on everybody else all the damn time."

In the early days of all this, I never did think too hard on any of it. Momma didn't have any use for mindless gossip and speculation. She tried real hard to keep me out of all of it. And eventually, all the supermarket chatter calmed down anyway.

That is, until the old town drunk was found dead, head cracked open, blood spilled all over the parking lot of Timecapsule's only bar. We just called it "The Bar," though I'm certain someone could tell you its name. Abernathy McClannahan was the drunk, though most just called him Old Abby.

It wasn't until a little after noon, after the sun had beaten down on him for a good half a day, that anyone knew he was there. They smelled him before they saw him. Musty, like a wet dog who rolled around in his own excrement with just a hint of whiskey.

The Bar's bartender, Matthias Wilcox, found him.

"Well, shit," Pa said as he hung up the phone.

"What?" I asked over my soggy bowl of over-sugared Wheaties.

"Mind your business and eat your cereal, kid."

Momma walked into the kitchen, still in her jammies, the pretty kind, under an aged terry cloth bathrobe. Pa leaned into her ear as her hand rested on his abdomen. "No shit," she said. "Old Abby?"

"So, I gotta go take a look and see what I can figure out."

Momma's hand moved to Pa's cheek, and she kissed his lips. I watched as he pulled away and a little trail of spittle kept them tethered a bit longer.

"Can I come? What happened to Old Abby?" I said, pushing away from the table.

"Breakfast, then school!" he replied.

"It's summer break."

"Well, in that case, no. You're out of your damn mind if you think you get a ride-along on this one." He put on his hat, the one that let you know he was sheriff of this town, and sauntered out of the kitchen. "Watch some TV. Rot your brain. And Goddamnit, stay inside."

I never did like being told what to do. But after a couple hours of staring out the window and chewing my nails down to nubs, I clicked on the TV. I flipped until I got to the midday news report, hoping there would be something about our little town to talk about. I listened impatiently as the weatherman told us it was going to be another scorcher out there. Then, lo and behold, a very blonde and hair-sprayed field reporter stood squinting right in front of The Bar.

"A little less than a month after a Hefty bag of trash killed a woman on Main Street here in Timecapsule, Tennessee, another local seems to have fallen victim to a mysterious bag of trash. Authorities are not releasing the name of the man but can confirm that the trash bag fell with enough force to kill him instantaneously. The contents of the bag included many empty glass beer bottles and several larger glass liquor bottles."

"That's what happened to old Abby," I said inadvertently out loud.

"On the news already, huh?" Momma said, a basket of laundry cradled on her hip. "Help me fold these."

I'd rather go outside. "Okay, Momma."

After Old Abby, everything started happening a lot faster. Pa got called away at all times of day and night, even on the weekends. Cartwright Davenport was victim number three. Smashed by a bag of dog toys and dishes on his own stoop on a Friday afternoon. Not sure if it was a water bowl to the head or the tumble down the stairs that did him in.

Ansel Partridge sat outside in the courtyard of the Sunny Time Timecapsule assisted living facility, having finally worked up the nerve to ask Miss Sharaldine Witherspoon, Timecapsule's own most wanted widow, to dinner. According to Sharaldine, he sat fidgeting with the hat in his hand, and before she could give him a response, BAM. Another garbage bag from the heavens came crashing down, and our little town was left scratching our collective heads. Sharaldine said her answer would have been yes, but maybe that's just because it's hard to tell a dead man no.

Laverne began to elaborate on her theory. "What if," she said, "just what if all of these accidents aren't accidents at all. They are divine intervention. The hand of God smiting the worst of us for our sins, leaving the rest little clues about what they could have done."

"Oh, really, Laverne? How can you even think such a thing?"

"Drunk Old Abby? Crushed by booze bottles! Cartwright? Dog toys. You know he shot his dog, don't you?"

"Bernard was old and dying. It was a mercy killing."

"Mercy killing or not, he murdered the old mutt."

"What about Ansel?"

"Sex toys!" Laverne shouted.

"Oh, Lord, Laverne. Ansel probably hasn't gotten it up in years." Patience was out of, well, patience for this kind of talk. "A little higher in the back."

"The higher the hair, the closer to Jesus."

"At least it will give a good buffer if I happen to get smitten by trash."

Patience did not get smitten by trash.

Instead, victim number five was another older gentleman from the Sunny Time Timecapsule. Almost as though it was a running gag in a movie or something, Preston VanDerZwagg was sitting on that same bench chatting up Miss Sharaldine Witherspoon, one in the same, as the largest bag of trash you've ever seen plummeted to the Earth. The bag was so big and so heavy, it broke that stone bench clean in half. Sharaldine sat there, speechless for a moment, and then all at once, as though she was taken by the Holy Spirit, she began convulsing and screaming. Words came out like they were choking her. "Trash. Dear God. Oh, God." Least, that's what I overheard.

That was the last straw for Pa, who met with Mayor Liverpool about a lockdown for the whole town. Anyone who could stay in was confined to their homes 24/7 until further notice, and those who must leave home, Godspeed.

"I just can't believe it," Momma said as she scooped extra mashed potatoes onto Pa's plate. "The exact same spot."

"Exactly."

"What I don't understand is how each of these bags seems to find a person. How is that even possible?"

"Oh, no," Pa responded, mouth full, "they're all over town. We keep picking 'em up in ditches, off rooftops. We sent a team to the city park. Found about 78 bags of random garbage. But for some reason, themed garbage. It's always crap that goes together."

"What's the best bag you found?" I asked

"Dolly!" Momma scolded.

But Pa didn't seem to mind. "Hmm," he puzzled, wiping the corner of his mouth with his thumb. "Well, I guess the other day, we picked up a bag of bubble wrap. All bubble wrap. Had to stop the guys in the station from popping it all."

Evidence, I thought.

"Evidence, you know."

"When do you think they are going to lift the quarantine? I'm getting antsy here."

"It's just not safe yet," Pa said softly, taking Momma's hand in his.

Only essential personnel were allowed out of their homes by mid-August. Just wasn't worth risking a bag of kitchen gadgets to the head or, well, a bag of shoes to your windshield. But when you're the sheriff, it's a risk you're expected to take.

So, when Pa got the call that Matthias Wilcox's six-year-old daughter, Gerssie, was flattened by another mystery bag while playing out in her backyard, Pa had to go. "Goddamnit. That's what the ban was for. So shit like this didn't happen to any Goddamn kids." He huffed and puffed as he pulled on his shoes. Momma stood over him, her hand on his shoulder. "Stay in the Goddamn house. Both of you."

"We will, baby." Momma pressed her mouth to his real hard. There was some kind of premonition in the way she lingered there. "Be safe."

"I gotta go." He said, but he wasn't moving. He just held her in his arms and with his eyes. "I love you."

"You come home safe, you hear me," she demanded, and then she pressed her lips so hard to his you would think his teeth might break. "I love you."

And like a hero in an action movie, he walked to the door, looked back for a moment, and pulled it closed behind him. I swear to God, I heard Momma let out the tiniest death gasp like she knew what was coming.

Hours passed.

Pa had never been gone this long. Usually it was a small team of people taking pictures, rifling through trash, zipping up body bags, and writing up a quick police report. But the afternoon was long gone, and the dark was creeping in. At first, Momma busied herself. Vacuuming, dusting, dishes, laundry, piling up items to take to the Goodwill in Fayetteville, and polishing the silver we've literally never used—until there was nothing left to do. I sat in Pa's chair reading a Hardy Boys novel from his childhood collection. Momma, now very lost, stood in the middle of the living room, arms folded across her chest, staring deeply into the carpet.

"I'm never going to get that spot out."

I followed her line of vision and noticed the faint purple spot she was fixed on. It was from one afternoon when Momma had been standing in that very spot, sipping an uncharacteristic glass of red wine while watching Ellen on the TV. Pa got home early and snuck up on her, which startled the wine glass right out of her hand. Pa laughed, but Momma was madder than the dickens. Red wine on her ivory carpet. She tried everything to get it out, but somehow, it was always going to be there. Suddenly, a knock at the door jolted her to the present. "Get on to bed, Dolly."

"Momma..."

"You heard me."

Now, a knock at the door was a good indication Pa wasn't home. It was also a pretty good indication that nothing good could be going on. I turned the corner down the hall to my room and pressed my body flat against the wall to listen in. I could hear Momma waiting. I think we were both waiting for the sky to fall. Another knock, then the thrust of the opening door.

"Mrs. McWallswart?" a deep male voice finally spoke.

"It's Day. Mags Day."

"Are you married to Danforth McWallswart?"

"Yes. I am."

Clearly these guys weren't from Timecapsule, or they would have known Momma, would have known she kept her maiden name because she wasn't from these parts either and McWallswart was just too much for her.

"I'm very sorry, ma'am, but we have some bad news for you," a woman's voice chimed in. That's when Momma broke into a million pieces of grief, right there in the doorway, hand still clutching the knob but crouched down on the ground.

I came back around the door. "Momma," but no one seemed to notice me.

Time stood still. The two officers—I would later learn were FBI—stood all stoic as Momma heaved sighs so heavy they could break a person. I just stood in the living room, looking on, standing right in the spot of the impossible stain, the one that would always be there.

So much of that night was a blur, but here's what we learned: Pa was headed out just west of town to the Willcox farmhouse where little Gerssie was crushed like a pancake by a bag of aquarium rubble, when another bag made impact with his car. Torpedoed right through the windshield. His car spun out of control and smashed right into a big old sugar maple, pinning him in. Hard to say what killed him, like that's what really matters here anyway. But many folks in town like to debate it.

"We're in hell here, Mags." Laverne handed Momma a cup of coffee that she wasn't going to drink and put her hand to her back. Momma had nothing to say.

"When's it gonna end?" Matthias asked. I wondered if he had even had time to wash his suit after his own daughter's funeral two days prior. Most of Timecapsule had too much cabin fever to postpone the funerals. "We can't just stay holed up inside forever."

"Excuse me," Momma replied and shuffled off down the hall to the bathroom.

"We've been cursed, that's for damn sure. Something evil is here in Timecapsule, and we have to do away with it." Laverne called after her.

"You really think we're being punished for something here, Laverne?" Patience Hollyhocks chirped.

"I do. It's all part of God's plan."

"God's plan," Matthias gasped. "You're telling me my child is dead because of some God's plan."

"And my Pa?" It just sort of toppled out of my mouth like an avalanche.

Laverne got all quiet for a moment, remembering herself. She set her cup of coffee down and said, "You tell your Momma her next haircut is on me," and she walked out.

The days passed slowly, and eventually, the sky stopped falling. No more reports of people dying, and no more random trash bags turned up around town. People started to leave their houses again, but you could see the hesitation in the tentative way everyone walked through town, always close to the buildings, faster if there was nothing overhead that might break a fall. Everyone was visibly pretty traumatized, but feeling in the clear, if not still very confused. Took weeks before any real answers came out.

See, it turns out, Pa was important enough to make the news outside of South Central Tennessee. That's how we found out it wasn't God's plan at all. After the body count was reported, a very repentant Nashville billionaire came forward to claim responsibility. "Drones," he said. He was using drones to drop odds and ends that he no longer needed or wanted in a place he thought no one would ever go. Timecapsule is so small, it doesn't pop up on most maps. So he thought it was the perfect, if not most flawed, way of disposing of his trash while also testing out his new delivery drones, the ones he planned to sell to Amazon when they begin the rollout of their drone delivery system. Only problem was, these drones now had a body count. And so did he.

Because the guy never meant to kill anyone, and he came forward, it all got settled out of court. He gave several million dollars to the city of Timecapsule for all the damages and the much-needed restoration to the infrastructure, and he shelled out an extra ten million to the families who lost someone in the—what he called—experiment.

When that check came in the mail, Momma held it in her arms the way she would have held Pa. "That's ours?" I asked.

"Yes," Momma replied.

"That's a lot."

"Yes."

"What are we going to do with it all?"

"I don't know," Momma told me, wrapping an arm around me and pulling me tight. "It can't do the one thing I need it to."

I knew what she meant. It wasn't Pa, and it was never going to be Pa. He was gone.

"What do you say we get the hell out of here?"

"What do you mean?" I asked, but I knew. Momma wanted to leave. Timecapsule was all I ever knew, but Momma, she knew there was more than this. She knew there were places where the sky never fell.

"That stain is never gonna come clean," Momma said.

I Am No Clown

by Randy L. Gross

I killed the Volkenstanders.

There, the confession is on record, and I have nothing more to say on the subject! Swear to me that you'll never ever bring it up again!

Now, if only my conscience would accept a vow of silence.

Yes, I killed the Volkenstanders, even if it wasn't in the strict biblical sense. I was only five at the time, and my little hands couldn't have fit around anyone's neck. Let alone a whole family's collective neck.

The Volkenstanders. Come on! You have to remember them. The Flying Volkenstanders, a troupe of aerial acrobats…trapeze artists. Renowned from Brownsville to El Paso for the six-and-a-half man pyramid, performed 100 feet in the air. They came after the Wallenda family, in case you're asking, but were no less spectacular. And like the Wallendas, they never used a net. That was their downfall, so to speak.

Or I was.

For the sake of clarification, I did not kill every single member of the high-wire family. But due to the Volkenstanders' inability to reproduce like rabbits (or Wallendas), the circus community pronounced them deader than road-killed armadillo the morning of August 14, 1964. That was the morning after my slip…and theirs.

Wait! Don't think for a moment that I am coming clean after nearly forty years in an attempt to cleanse my soul. I asked Mama, God rest her good heart, and Dad, the bastard, for forgiveness before I went to bed that night. Repeatedly. With tears coursing down my cheeks. How else could I have fallen asleep? And I would have gladly gone to jail or a juvenile detention home—hell, even permanent internment at summer camp—if someone, anyone, could have prevented me from going through adolescence.

Four life sentences, served consecutively, that's all I was asking for. Even concurrently, I didn't care. Better yet, four death sentences for the murders of Lugar, Lonnie, Erika, and Fredrich Volkenstander. Pretty heady stuff for a five-year-old, huh? But I deserved it, I assure you, as much as any infantile killer in the annals of crime.

But then, all killers are infantile, if you ask me.

It was the week after my fifth birthday, and circus tickets were a belated gift from my father. He was a good man, as far as bastards go, and didn't mean to forget my birthday. Sure, sometimes he liked to pretend that I'd never been born, but then so did I.

"Don't be an idiot," he screamed at me, pulling his steel-toed clodhoppers over woolen gray socks. "Elephants are born and raised to be in the circus!"

I had merely commented that it seemed cruel to chain and shackle any living creature, let alone one that was fifty times bigger than us, and asked if the rumors were true about captive elephants going mad and crushing their trainers.

"If that had happened," continued my father, "do you think there'd still be elephants in the circus? I oughtta—"

He lowered his hand as soon as my mother entered the room. Mama was a looker, and that never changed. Whatever makes a beautiful woman go for a pot-bellied pig of a man like my dad, I'll never know. Beauty calms the savage beast even more than music.

"Hey, little buddy," shouted my father energetically, smiling while engaged in the impromptu act of giving me a noogie. "If we're lucky tonight, we may get to see the maromeros."

The maromeros. That's what my father liked to call the acrobats. He always told everyone he was from Mexico, but he spoke few words in his "native" language. Unless you count the four-letter variety.

"The acrobats are fun," said Mama, "especially the aerialists. But there's still nothing that tops the clowns. Did I ever tell the story about the first time my poppa took me to see the clowns?"

"We don't have time for that," shouted Dad, a fleck of his lunchtime beans and rice (don't ask me which one) hurtling and landing on the collar of Mama's spiffy blue dress. "The carpa is twenty miles from here, and if I miss the start, I'm asking for my money back!"

Mama's stories were always very entertaining. When I got older, I wished she would have written down a few of them, maybe published them in a book. But Dad never had the patience for them and certainly never offered any encouragement. In a year that saw the Beatles invade America, Martin Luther King Jr. win a Nobel Peace Prize, and Arnold Palmer win a fourth Masters, you would have thought people would have been seeing more promise in one another.

It was also the year that China exploded its first A bomb, the Soviet Union started using spy satellites, Jimmy Hoffa got convicted for jury tampering, and a stampede killed three hundred spectators at a soccer game in Peru. I only mention the last item because I feel in my gut that I caused the stampede to happen. Or at least my doppelganger did. The kid in the newspaper photo fleeing the stadium gates certainly looked like my twin. He had that same twisted grin.

It was the expression I bore every time I rode the Ferris wheel or climbed the steps to one of those outdoor observation decks. Open stairways and open air terrified me, to the point where I felt like jumping. That would, after all, be the quickest way back to solid ground. My mama's brother, Uncle Boozer, did take flight one blustery January night in New York City. The story that's told says a broken heart sent him feet first off the roof of the Empire State Building. But, the truth is, it was gambling debts that sent him off the roof of a one-story Walgreens. If he hadn't landed on his head, he would have survived.

I was all grins when I first stepped foot inside the carpa. For a five-year-old, a circus tent might as well be the Taj Mahal. It's a mystical, almost mythical kind of experience, sort of like stumbling upon the hanging gardens of Babylon. That first time…always the most memorable time, of course. But then, I would never have anything to compare it to.

It was also one of those rare occasions when my father and I would actually agree on something.

Sure, the clowns were pretty cool, and out of respect to my mother, I outwardly displayed more enthusiasm for the Mr. Slick and Smooth Guy imitators than I was truly feeling inside. Besides, they weren't clowns in the technical sense, but rather what fans of the carpas affectionately referred to as pelado. Translated into English, these so-called clowns were underdogs, stock characters who performed sketches dealing with human foibles and scandals. Mama laughed at the way the pelado used their wits to survive.

Dad and I were there for one reason, and one reason only. We just had to see the famous six-and-a-half man pyramid, a high-wire masterpiece performed by four male Volkenstanders, two female Volkenstanders, and the official Flying Volkenstander mascot (hence the half-man): a professionally costumed and coiffured Chihuahua by the name of Blix.

"You should be a clown," Mama gushed as the final pelado finished taking his bows in ring number one. "It is so important in life for people to laugh at life."

"And what kind of career would that be," Dad retorted. "How can he ever support his old man on a pelado's salary?"

I wasn't truly listening to either one of my parents. The spotlight had just now vanished like a genie, only to reappear in ring three, where two towering telephone poles rose the whole way to the top of the roof, and a taut cable stretched from one pole to the other. The ringmaster was calling for the crowd's attention—my attention! My tiny heart was thumping inside my chest, outdistancing the pace of the timpani's mounting drum roll.

Ladies and gentlemen…presenting the masters of all maromeros, the high-flying kings and queens of the sky…the Flying Volkenstanders!

The applause was ear-shattering. I remember thinking, "What must it feel like to be so well-loved!" I wanted a piece of this pie in the sky, to wash it down with a tall glass of cold milk and then eat some more.

Sweet things always have been a weakness of mine. Did I mention how much I like caramel corn? I was holding a jumbo cardboard carton of it, cradled between my legs so I could use my hands to clap, as the Flying Volkenstanders entered ring three and acknowledged their fans with a simultaneous wave of their hands.

No flash cameras, please! The admonishing voice from somewhere near the top of the tent roof could have been the ringmaster's, but my five-year-old imagination likened it to God's.

Complete and utter silence. This time, the words seemed to come from Fredrich Volkenstander, the patriarch of the acrobatic troupe, as he announced the feat that was mere moments away: the highlight of the evening, the famous six-and-a-half-man pyramid! Surely nothing could ever beat this, I thought, stuffing caramel corn into my mouth with rapid expectation. "Just wait till I tell Grandpa."

My mom's old man wasn't around all that much, but I wished he had been. Grandpa liked me, and he was the closest thing to a role model I would ever have.

You could have heard a penny drop from the hole in my pocket and fall into my sneaker—that's how hushed the crowd was as Lugar and Lonnie Volkenstander stepped out onto the tightrope from one end, while Gunther and Greta Volkenstander (the latter being a real "bruiser" of a woman) stepped from the opposite platform. A sturdy horizontal pole with dual shoulder bars was then lifted above their heads, and the four performers became linked.

The acrobatic plot thickened then. Could you believe it? A bicycle was now placed upon the horizontal pole, ably guided there by Fredrich Volkenstander, who himself was guided by a balancing stick. And once he was completely balanced—on wheels!—in the middle of the emerging pyramid, scantily-clad Erika Volkenstander (in retrospect, probably the real reason why my dad liked the maromeros so much) walked gingerly to where her father was, and climbed atop his shoulders. How stupendous!

I felt like clapping, but restrained myself. I sensed Dad shifting his weight in his seat, subconsciously moving his hips in sympathetic sync with Erika's efforts to maintain her balance. Mama gasped, but quickly covered her mouth with an embroidered handkerchief. Silence can be tough under climactic duress.

Then just think how tough it was now. Every sundae needs a cherry on top, right? Well, every six-and-a-half-man pyramid needs its half-a-man too, and from out of a crocheted bag hanging tightly below Erika Volkenstander's shimmering breasts came Blix, the wonder dog. Or a reasonable facsimile thereof. Yes, Blix wasn't moving (and when have you ever seen a Chihuahua stand still?). He wasn't a real dog at all, but rather a costumed and coiffured shadow of his former self who owed his prolonged existence to a taxidermist.

Swiftly and dexterously, Erika placed a tiny pedestal atop her head, then Blix "the pretend wonder dog" atop the pedestal, and just like that, history was made!

Boy was it ever.

Long-distance vertigo began to consume me. My heart was clamoring, not only in my ears, but my whole sinus cavity. I was breathing in short, shallow bursts. In my mind's eye's, that was me up there on the tightrope. That was me, teetering like a top on a string. That was me, suddenly looking for the quickest way back to solid ground. Inside my head, I was shouting at myself, "Jump…jump!"

Only it wasn't inside my head.

I have no idea how many times I bellowed before Dad slapped his hand over my mouth. But three thousand and four finger-pointing eyes were simultaneously focused on me, however briefly, before the chain reaction began.

I believe beautiful Erika started it. Her whole body shook when I screamed, and before she could realign her hips, Blix had fallen from its pedestal and tumbled into Fredrich's lap. You would have thought that the senior Volkenstander would have been prepared for anything, but having a dog between his legs—albeit a stuffed dog—caused him to lose control of his bike and go careening, back and forth, from one end of the horizontal pole to the other.

Erika hung on, God bless her. And the anchors—Lugar, Lonnie, Gunther, and Greta—almost pulled off the most amazing bit of counterbalancing ever accomplished one hundred feet above the ground. But by now, utter chaos had broken out in the Big Top. Panic was contagious. People could feel catastrophe brewing in their bones, and it takes an awful lot of skill to oppose such a collective doom-mongering.

Gunther and Greta were the only ones lucky enough to avoid falling. Actually, Gunther did fall, but Greta was able to catch the wire on her descent and catch Gunther's wrist during his. A rescue net was erected just in time to save them both. A rescue net erected over-top the broken bodies of the four Volkenstanders whom I had killed.

The lights over the Big Top shine no more. The show is over, the crowds are gone…the Flying Volkenstanders are dead.

That's what the lead story on the front page of the daily newspaper said the following day. Hell, it could have been a perpetual headline every day for forty years, the way I see it.

I would never become a clown. To be a class clown, you need to be loud, even crass, and to accomplish either requires a voice. All through my grade-school days, I was unable to speak above a whisper. Teachers taking roll call would mark me absent, and my parents grew tired of visits from the local truant officer. In school plays, I was habitually cast in the demanding roles of Tree, Sun, or (my personal favorite) Tumbleweed. On Career Day, when counselors would ask me what I wanted to be when I grew up, I would mouth the words "inanimate object." On playgrounds, kids would play their games of Marco Polo and Olly Olly Oxen Free sans me.

I yearned to redeem myself. I wanted to entertain. As a teenager, I began to imitate Marcel Marceau. But mime wasn't the only thing I dabbled in. Contortionism seemed like a natural extension of my deathly silent persona. It truly felt good bending over backwards for a semi-appreciative audience.

My father threatened to break my back when he first saw me perform. That's why I left home when I was seventeen and started living in the streets. If you ask me, that's where some of the world's most talented entertainers live. And trust me when I say that man can live on bread alone, as long as there's an occasional dab of grape jelly to satisfy his sweet tooth. I survived on little more than jelly sandwiches for twenty odd years, honing and then plying my craft for mere quarters and dimes. Until one day, it happened. You know…the "f" word.

Sort of.

Have you ever seen a mime/contortionist? Most people haven't, which explains why my cash bucket was starting to fill more rapidly. People must have been driving for miles around to see me perform, because new faces were in abundance. I felt proud. Even ecstatic.

That is, until I overheard an old geezer exclaim, "Bring on the maromeros! I miss the maromeros! I miss the Volkenstanders!"

Was it my "dear" old dad's haggard voice? I can't say for sure. But hearing the name of my victims sparked something in my head. It was an uncontrollable urge. Put simply, I opened my mouth wide and started screaming. After nearly fifteen years of abject silence, I began wailing like a banshee. And not just any old words. No, I began yelling obscenities that most people don't know exist. In English, in Spanish, in freaking German. I was shouting in tongues…a full-blown, rip-snortin' screaming rampage that lasted for at least fifteen minutes, echoing throughout the streets of Laredo and disturbing folks' late suppers and family TV hours.

How did they react? Like I was a homicidal maniac, that's how. All it took was for one good ol' bubba in bib overalls to grab a pitchfork, and before you knew it, half the town was chasing after me with more pitchforks. And tire irons. And cans of kerosene. It was like some kind of Frankenstein movie, and not even good enough to earn a grade of B.

Much to my dismay, they hounded me all the way to a tenement building, where my only recourse was to escape to the roof. I was pushed to the edge, step by step, by a rising tide of Laredo loons. Or a riptide, with more bargaining power than any police interrogation room. I certainly wasn't going to jump, so…I confessed! To every crime against humanity I could think of! The assassination of Kennedy! The kidnapping of Patty Hearst! The Jonestown Massacre! Hell, I even accepted responsibility for the hole in the ozone layer.

And last, but not least, the murder of the Volkenstanders.

At least the judge was lenient. He was one of those ahead-of-his-times liberals who adored creative sentencing. "If you like to entertain, then that's precisely what you will do," he ordered with a half-smirk. "As a trapeze artist with the Mexican circus!"

Needless to say, I do a lot of traveling nowadays. My legs aren't shackled, but I wear one of those ankle bracelets. And I'm a veritable poster boy for fearlessness. That's me, look way up there—one hundred feet in the air in perfect balance, walking slowly, one foot in front of the other while hundreds, if not thousands, of mothers, fathers, and their kids watch in advised silence. Kids probably like me.

Whatever you do, please don't ask me to jump.

And never ever bring this up again.

Crossed Lines

by B.W. Jackson

The sun was shining when the new neighbors arrived. They had one yappy dog and one little girl with wiry arms, wiry legs, and wiry hair. Raymond watched them from his dining room window. The mother waved to Raymond.

No one had been in the neighborhood longer than Raymond Butterley. He had been in his house at the end of the cul-de-sac for thirty years. He did not talk to new neighbors until they had stayed for three years. He did not want to waste his time with the kind of people who left a house after just a couple years.

The neighborhood was his kingdom. He had a view of every parcel of land from his kitchen window. The Pfeiffers, a young couple a few houses down, saluted him every time they left the house. That was the type of fidelity he expected. No. That was the type of fidelity he demanded.

#

His new neighbors had gotten off to a good start. The mother had waved, and she continued to wave from time to time when she saw Raymond sitting at his big rectangular kitchen window. The father pretended not to see Raymond. The neighbors were called Thornton.

Fall arrived, and then winter. The following spring, Raymond saw Mrs. Thornton. She emerged from the side door of her house, as a squirrel emerges from a nut lair. Raymond sat up straight with his cup of coffee. She was carrying a large spade with a pink handle. Raymond stood up and went to the side window just in time to see Mrs. Thornton stand up on the spade. He set down his coffee on the floor and walked outside.

"That's my property," he said.

Mrs. Thornton looked up and down the invisible property line. Raymond walked right up to her. He pulled her spade out of the ground and kicked the upset dirt back into the hole.

"You see this tree?" he said.

She looked up at the tall, unsteady pine tree.

"That's the one," he said. "You're crossing the line."

"Oops," said Mrs. Thornton. "I guess we've just got our lines crossed."

She smiled. She poked Raymond in the ribs. He slapped her hand.

"You can say that again," he muttered.

"I said, 'I guess we've just got our lines crossed.'"

"I said, 'You can say that again.'"

"I did!"

Mrs. Thornton guffawed, and her guffaw turned into a hearty laugh.

"Are you done?" said Raymond.

"What?"

"Never mind."

Raymond walked back to his porch. Mrs. Thornton called after him.

"I'm not talking to you for another two years," Raymond said.

"Are you cross with me?" yelled Mrs. Thornton. "Get it?"

Raymond shook his head. She laughed again, even more loudly. He opened his door and kicked over his coffee.

#

The next morning, Raymond drank his coffee in the living room instead of the kitchen. He stared out the window into the side yard. Just as he expected, Mrs. Thornton appeared in the middle of the morning. This time she had her wiry little girl with her. They dug another hole a few feet away from the first hole, and another hole, and another hole. When the wiry little girl stepped backwards onto Raymond's property, he rapped on the glass with his knuckles. In total, they dug eight holes.

In the afternoon, Mrs. Thornton and the wiry little girl went out in their minivan. Raymond went to his garage. He filled up a bucket of rock salt. He poured two cups of salt in all eight holes. He went back to his chair at the kitchen window and waited. The minivan appeared an hour later. Behind the sliding door were eight small shrubs. He sipped his coffee. He went to the living room window.

The expression on Mrs. Thornton's face delighted Raymond.

The mother got a bucket. The child got a little spade. They shoveled the salt out of all eight holes as Raymond watched. They planted the shrubs one by one. The wiry little girl was a pretty good worker.

#

The wiry little girl knocked on his door.

"Mr. Butterley?"

"Yep."

"Do you want to come to dinner?"

"What?"

"I made you an invitation."

She held out a folded piece of paper. He took it out of her hand and unfolded it.

"Don't they teach penmanship any more?"

"No."

"I can tell."

The girl looked at her feet.

"Got anything else to say?"

"No."

"I'll see you tomorrow night."

In the late afternoon, Raymond carried over a melamine plate to the Thornton house. He rang the doorbell. The girl answered.

"I'll take it to go."

The girl said nothing. Her father appeared in an apron.

"I want it to go," said Raymond.

"Well," said Mr. Thornton. "Okay."

Raymond held out the plate. Mr. Thornton nodded. He took the plate. He hesitated.

"But, you see, the rice isn't ready."

"I can wait."

"Okay."

Mr. Thornton disappeared into the kitchen with the plate. Raymond stood in the doorway. The girl stood with her hand on the door. Mrs. Thornton came down the stairs.

"Oh. Hello."

"Hello."

Mrs. Thornton stood in the front hall. She breathed through her mouth.

"Won't you come in?"

"No."

"No?"

"No."

Mrs. Thornton looked at her daughter.

"No?"

"No."

"Well, then," said Mrs. Thornton. "I'll be right back."

They whispered in the kitchen. They returned with a plate. The portion sizes were modest, Raymond thought.

"Mr. Butterley," said Mrs. Thornton, "we wanted to ask you something."

"That's how it always is."

"Well, we wanted to have you for dinner."

"Sure."

"But we also wanted to ask you about the tree."

"What tree?"

"The pine tree."

"What about it?"

"You may have noticed we had a tree man here."

"I did."

"He is worried about the tree. He thinks it could fall any day now."

"Looks healthy to me."

"Yes. Wait. What?"

"That tree has always been that way."

"You see," said Mr. Thornton. "According to the tree man, the tree is liable to fall, and it is liable to fall on our house."

"Why do you say that word?"

"What word?"

"Liable."

"Mr. Butterley."

"I am not liable for that tree."

"I was not saying you were."

"I know exactly what you were saying."

Raymond took his plate of food from Mr. Thornton. He pulled the door away from the wiry little girl and closed it behind him.

The chicken was good, but the rice was undercooked, Raymond decided.

#

At the end of the summer, the tree man returned. Raymond was ready. He dragged a plastic chair over to the pine tree. He plugged in an orange extension cord and unwound it out to the tree. He went back to the garage for his leaf blower.

The tree man wandered the yard before approaching the pine tree.

"Good afternoon, sir."

Raymond turned on the leaf blower.

"Sir?"

Raymond aimed the leaf blower at the tree man and pulled the trigger. He blew air in his face. The tree man closed his eyes and scrunched up his face. He stepped away. Raymond took his finger off the trigger.

"Sir?"

Raymond said nothing.

"I was hoping to talk to you about this tree."

Raymond said nothing. The tree man slowly approached again.

"I thought we could have a conversation."

Raymond blew air in his face. The tree man closed his eyes and nodded as he backed away.

#

In the early fall, a big storm came through. In the middle of the night, the wind howled and howled. Across the neighborhood, branches shook and bows swayed. Raymond woke up and went to the window. He stared at the old pine. The tree creaked back and forth. Beyond the tree, the light flicked on at the Thornton house. Mrs. Thornton appeared in the window. Raymond went back to bed.

In the morning, all the neighbors were wandering the street, inspecting the damage. A small crowd had gathered at the end of the cul-de-sac. Mrs. Thornton and Mr. Thornton and their wiry little girl went outside. They stood in the street. The tree had fallen in the center of the roof. The old pine had karate-chopped the house in half.

The wiry little girl walked up to the house and rang the doorbell. But Raymond Butterley was dead.

The Trapper and the Great Golden Rabbit

by Granville de Shinka

Far into what is now called the American North, there are vast expanses of thick evergreen forests ranging hundreds of miles—over mountains, between rivers, crowding valleys. For the people who made this terrain their home, the immense forestland was an altar deserving reverence for having housed and outlived every ancestor—a great mother nurturing millions of people for twice as many years, providing for, protecting, and, when so moved, punishing those who knew themselves by relation to the forest. Persons of these tribes learned life lessons through chores and routines aimed toward survival, yet did not merely survive, but thrived inside this roaming acreage. Somewhat unfortunately, this story is not about them, who for so long lived in harmony with nature, but the ancient woodlands itself.

A French trapper walked along a mountain stream. He had departed from the trading post of Deschamps three days earlier and was on his way to the trading post of Champlain, described by those at Deschamps as "three days northeast following the silent stream." Having traveled the majority of the journey, the trapper smelled bonfires a ways off. He would have seen smoke in the sky, too, if not for the towering forest all around him.

Stopping to scoop cold, clear water in his cupped hands, the trapper spotted a golden rabbit across the stream, less than twenty paces from him. Not a yellow rabbit, nor a rabbit powdered in sand or dust, but a rabbit glittering with the brilliance of polished gold. Frozen on his haunches and unthinking, icy water escaping through cracks between fingers and falling to rejoin the creek's peaceful whisper, the trapper fell into a trance induced by the golden rabbit.

The rabbit continued without concern for the trapper, intermittently sniffing the sparse vegetation that sprouted after a winter longer and colder than any in living memory. It hopped to a fallen tree that lay across the waters, then disappeared into its hollow trunk. This severance of sight, from hunter to prize, roused the trapper from warm half-visions.

"Now that is a creature of spectacle. All I could do with its pelt!" gleamed the trapper.

He wiped his hands on his bearskin coat and pulled on a pair of beaver mittens. "I would have a most fantastic hat made from it, or else, present it as a token to the Queen. I would achieve legendary status and be met with admiration wherever I went!" The trapper smiled absently, stroking his matted beard.

He rose and approached the fallen tree, taking seeds from his pack with which to tempt the rabbit. It did not reemerge since entering the felled tree and, therefore, thought the trapper, must still be in it. The trapper placed a pile of seeds at the end closest to him, then, scurrying across on the top of the tree, he did the same, placing bait on the other side where the rabbit vanished a short time before. The trapper unsheathed his hunting knife and took to rapping on the hollow trunk, hoping to stir the rabbit.

Nothing.

For many minutes, the trapper knelt atop the trunk, halfway between the banks of the stream and piles of seeds, knife in hand, tapping the trunk every so often, waiting. He chided his mind whenever it strayed from its singular, glorious goal to notice the sludgy clumps of snow that fell from the forest's canopy. He swiveled his head from seed-pile to seed-pile. He suspected the stream had sped up since he began his journey three days earlier, perhaps even since he spotted the gold rabbit. He went on waiting, and more water droplets charged down the slopes of the melting mountaintops as the seasons progressed.

Seed-pile to seed-pile, from thought to adjacent thought, the trapper's lateral movements during the prolonged period of total concentration worked up a sweat beneath his fur garments. He removed his coonskin cap and wiped his face with it, swooped to submerge it in the cold water, and placed it back on his head. Just then, he heard movement within the trunk. Eyes narrow, jaw tensed, he sought a glimpse of his golden-furred mark.

He heard the subtle shift of seeds on the side of the stream he first saw the rabbit on. In a stealthy flash, the trapper was down where the pile had been, looking into the hollow tree, reaching desperately at the abyss his gold rabbit hid within. Frustrated, he did this for too many seconds. Accepting, eventually, that few trappers ever caught their prey blindly, he cursed and stood to begin planning his next move.

He cursed louder and spat involuntarily when he discovered the other seeds had vanished also. He walked on the tree across the stream and looked down at his scheme's sorry legacy: an impression in the dirt. He glanced over his shoulder in time to see a gold tuft bounce back into the trunk.

Furious, he now screamed his curses and other sounds that were meaningless and more animalistic. The trapper threw his hat and gloves and pack on the forest floor, close to where he had stopped to drink from the stream a half hour before. It felt a lifetime ago—or a different life altogether—when he stopped to rest en route to Champlain and the golden rabbit declared itself to him. Its appearance upended the entirety of his life; thirty-six years of folly were instantaneously made irrelevant. The inexplicable rabbit seemed the reason why he roamed the dense forests of the New World, why he was anywhere…why he was at all.

Then the trapper heard snickering wash in from around him. He spun slowly on the log, scoping the forest, trying to find whomever it was that took such hearty pleasure at his expense.

"Show yourself, coward!"

The snickering subsided without the trapper learning its source.

The trapper, being a proud man who derived this considerable pride chiefly from his abilities as a woodsman and hunter, took these taunts as attacks on his honor. He decided that if his mocker would not dare show themself, then he must catch the golden beast, to at once put an end both to the rabbit's trickery and the ridicule of his unseen tormenter. In a rush of related emotions, the trapper felt then that he'd rather die than leave without the opulent pelt. He could not bear to continue with only the tale of an uncatchable golden creature that nobody would believe existed anyway, when the actual breathing fact of the thing was just below him, holed up in a hollow log.

He returned to his pack, and from a shirt, he fastened two veils. He tied these tight on the ends of the fallen tree, covering the only points of entry and escape. Then he sat on the middle of the log and started to drill into the bark with his blade. He sat this way for hours, rubbing the handle of the hunting knife between his palms, wooden dust falling into the log or stream, slowly expanding a hole wide enough to reach his entire arm into, so as to grab the insolent rabbit by its golden hide and reclaim his precious dignity.

As the hole grew and the sun set, the trapper perceived a shaft of golden light emanating from the trunk. This translucent ray had the strange, elusive quality of a rainbow. Reinvigorated by wonderment, he took to stirring his blade on the edges of the hole, scraping away fine sheets with each revolution, switching hands when tired.

Over the following moments, the woods darkened, the hole widened, the brilliant ray became ever more apparent, and the trapper's enthusiasm grew to a fever pitch. He long had forgotten the mysterious laughter from the woods. He jabbed the knife in the bark and again washed his hands and face in the stream's frigid waters.

The woods were utterly dark, besides the magnificent gold light and stars above shining dimly through the forest's density. He plunged his greedy arm into the gap he had carved out, blocking the gold light and further darkening his already indistinct surroundings.

Immediately, the unclaimed laughter returned. Now, however, it was a booming, bloodcurdling hysteria. The trapper's arm recoiled, and his spine shuddered. The sweat that rolled down his back was as icy as the stream below him. Fearing physical attack, he scampered to his pack to retrieve his flintlock and lantern. The lantern's oil was low, but it had enough for an hour or so. The trapper prayed it would be enough to complete the mythic hunt and reach Deschamps before the gates were locked for the night.

He shoved the flintlock in his belt and stepped atop the log once more, propping the lantern against the base of a broken branch. He was alert and on guard for many minutes, until he had again put to the back of his mind the terrible laughter whose source he knew not. He sat, mesmerized by the light from the log's interior, and questioned the day's majesty and madness.

What was clear to him was that he was different now than when he had awoken. His inner truth became estranged from its notion of the man he believed himself to be, and the world became estranged from his understanding of it. And though he knew very well that he was the same as ever—the same animal and the same animate force—the trapper was certain somehow that on this day, his life had been irreparably altered. It was as if he jumped the tracks when he knelt to drink from the cold, quiet stream and the rabbit shone across it; as if fate revealed its face to him, but he was too close to discern anything significant, anything besides the creeping awareness of a domineering sneer. He did not know why, but it occurred to him then that the sneer must belong to the universe.

"Fine," he said aloud, to himself as much as the rabbit, to the woods' laughter as much as the universe itself. "I will do it, nevertheless, you great oaf. I will endure your scorn and the scorn of any that dare take this prize from me. I cannot leave this place having come so far, regretting what I so nearly accomplished. I will be the golden pelt's owner, or nothing at all!"

With renewed resolve, the trapper returned to his work. Expecting to learn where exactly in the log the rabbit cowered, he lowered his face to the light. The hole he'd carved fit almost his entire head and came up to his ears. But instead of coming face to face with that rabbit of gold radiance, the trapper saw nothing. However, the "nothing" he saw did not have the nothingness of Nothing. It was a reddish, opaque cloth that engulfed his vision. Like closing one's eyes and turning up to the sunny sky, he saw that red plane, shallow and endlessly deep, which results from the shut-eyed apprehension of immense energy.

Perplexed, gasping, the trapper took his face from the breach. The light beamed again from the fallen tree, incredibly brighter and more perfect. The trapper grabbed his knife from the bark and scraped the outskirts of the hole. Again, thin wooden shards fell into the log and the stream, and again, he plunged the blade back in the bark. Once more, the trapper lowered his head into the cutout cavity.

The golden aura returned to red void as he submerged his face in the hollow log, yet the trapper strained farther down, thinking of the rabbit's matchless fur. He felt the crevice pinch the folds of his ears, the curve of his chin, the crown of his head. Still, he pushed into the wooden chasm. The extra swipes from his blade allowed him to push his head all the way into the log with a pop. Then, the reddish void vibrated at a million points, and he watched as the vibrating specks began to spin ferociously, shooting in every direction, pulling the void taut, and finally tearing to reveal a bright other world.

This world was smaller than the void. The far edges were seamless curves, and the trapper realized he was inside a great orb—white on the brinks, next devolving into shades of blue, then evolving shades of green, and in the center, a golden oasis, also spherical. At the center of this golden oasis sat his golden rabbit, enormous, on an ornate, matching throne. Despite being in the dazzling world's periphery, his head jutted into it such that the trapper was level—(small, frightened) face to (gargantuan, grinning) face—with the Great Golden Rabbit.

"Bonjour, Pierre," the rabbit spoke, not with its mouth but from its world.

The trapper was aghast. The rabbit's glowing-ember eyes bored into him.

"Why are you here?" the Great Golden Rabbit asked.

The trapper tried to answer, but words failed. He thought briefly about begging for his release, but then remembered, to his horror, it was he who had gotten his head stuck in this world from his mistakes in the one he belonged to, on the other side of the red veil of nothingness, his world that failed upon mere sight of a golden rabbit.

He cautioned a yank of his neck. The orb world rippled with his effort. He realized he could still feel his body in his world—numb hands clutching the log's bark, knees hard against it, his arms shot out in search of the knife.

"What were you after, Pierre?" the Great Golden Rabbit pressed.

The innocence of the mocking question sent the desperate trapper into a rage. "Your fur! You know I wanted your fur! Do not pretend you don't know why I chased after you, why I trapped you!"

"Hmmmm," the Great Golden Rabbit rumbled, leaning back in his throne. "How do I appear to you?"

"What?!" the trapper jolted. "How do you 'appear' to me? Like a great golden rabbit, you fool! You are a golden rabbit!"

"It is interesting what people see. I have been said to be many things: a lake, a tree, both woman and man, even a dagger. But you, Pierre, you see a rabbit," grinned the Great Golden Rabbit.

At the mention of a dagger, the crazed trapper returned to searching for his knife. His hand swung back and forth about where he stabbed the bark. The trapper thought it must be just beyond his restricted reach.

"Now, Pierre, you got farther than most. For that, you deserve something special."

The trapper was a frenzy of fear. He strained his neck with all his might, sending more ripples through the orb world of the Great Golden Rabbit. The rabbit ignored it. It went on staring blankly at the disembodied trapper.

The trapper stretched his arm as far as he possibly could, his shoulder strained in pain, and swung near where he put the knife. Suddenly, his middle finger struck the knife's handle, and from a great distance, he heard the silent stream splash. The trapper leaked a pitiful groan. The rabbit's grin turned to a smirk.

"What do you think you deserve, Pierre?"

"Mercy!" the trapper cried.

"No, not that. Certainly not that." The Great Golden Rabbit leaned forward in his great golden throne and brought its face right up to the trapper's. "Can you think of anything else?"

"Death!" the trapper screamed into the monstrous face. He could hardly watch the rabbit's smirk become a horrible sneer. Laughter resounded through the orb world, through the halls of Pierre's spirit—a cascading, overlapping cacophony of madness. He writhed in terror and wished he would faint.

"Very well," the realm replied, the rabbit's sneer never ceasing.

The trapper fainted then. When his head lost consciousness in one world, his body went limp in the other. His knees slid from under him, and the flintlock went off, tearing through his thigh and fracturing his femur. As blood escaped the wound, his arms flailed about, knocked over the lantern, and doused his clothes in oil. Through the gunshot and the fire that spread over the log, the trapper did not regain consciousness. Flames consumed the log and the trapper whose head was stuck inside it. Blood ran; fire grew. The scorching heap weakened, collapsed, and fell into the stream. When it did, the fire extinguished, and as the awful mess sunk in the ice-cold water, it dissipated with a golden shimmer and faded from the forest's memory.

Along the stream, the trapper's pack remained, thrown in excitement on its bank. Beside the pack, with a few strewn items of clothing, an unmarked gold coin lied in the dirt.

The Holes in Everything

by Jason Arias

"The Broken Accordion"

Uncle Teddy's never been so quiet for so long. He'd liked silence so little that he tried to fill every bit of it up. Mom used to say that Teddy had been that way since they were little, that he could be too much sometimes, but she wouldn't have traded having a brother for anything, not even the quiet.

"Do you wish you had a brother?" she once asked me when I was younger.

"Girls don't need brothers to take care of them anymore, Mom."

"Hey, watch it!" Teddy roared, "You can't take that from me."

Teddy joked loud, laughed, and talked loud. He struck up conversations with strangers in line at the grocery store, with the neighbor's dog, with the TV. Sometimes Teddy would sing to himself in his booming baritone. But for the last week, Teddy hasn't said anything. I'm afraid that this is the new Teddy, that someday I may completely forget what he sounds like.

"You can't take that from me," I whisper over Teddy's body in the hospital bed. My hand looks tiny laying on his bony knuckles. His hands are still huge, but his body looks so much smaller than it used to be. Like somebody has deflated him. I pull my hair from my chin and tuck it behind my ear.

There's a machine on the opposite side of the bed that breathes for Teddy because his brain isn't sending the signal to his lungs anymore. The machine that's breathing for Teddy sounds like I imagine a broken accordion would sound being squeezed.

I imagine that Mom is still with me in ghost form, that she's playing the broken accordion machine and keeping the steady rhythm that makes Teddy's chest go up and down. Like the three of us are still together. Even if we're all irreversibly transformed and broken in different ways, we're together.

Teddy doesn't look as broken as he'd looked right after the incident, but somehow the machine and the hospital bed and the off-sterile smell feels more grotesque than the incident itself. I keep trying to use the word incident. I'm getting better at it. Incident is a term used to separate ourselves from our feelings. It's a term I'd like to use more convincingly.

The breathing machine and the beeping and Teddy's general unkemptness are heartbreaking, but even heartbreaking isn't the right word. In a world where everything is literally falling (and figuratively falling) apart, you should be prepared for every fracture before it happens. I should be crunching numbers with people smarter than me, trying to devise a way to prevent anomalous gravity deaths, trying to prevent the sky from cracking and letting objects from our past land on us.

Instead, I'm distracted by how much off-white tape there is everywhere.

There's tape wrapped around the breathing tube coming out of Teddy's mouth and stuck in V formations to the sides of his stubbled face. There's tape holding IV tubes in place over the veins on his forearms. Manila tape is pulled tight around the one-way valve sticking out of the hole the doctors made in Teddy's head. The way the tape on his head is peeling back from around the valve gives the appearance of the tiniest, grossest children's "Happy Birthday" party cone hat ever.

I don't want tape to be the last thing I remember about Teddy.

I feel like I should tell all the stupid jokes Teddy ever told me, back to him. Like, by me doing that, we could reverse the curse put on his brain. But I can't remember any of his jokes right now, and I know brains don't work like that. If you want to save somebody, you have to think less magically and more practically, like a mechanic instead of a magician. I need to focus on the plumbing instead of the paranormal.

Teddy's first day in the ER, after the CT scan came back, the doctor pulled me aside and said, "We need to relieve the intracranial pressure." He paused to pat at the top of his head. "We're basically going to burp your uncle's brain. Don't worry, we do this all the time."

"I understand," I said.

"Right," the doctor said. "Right."

The specialist came in on his off day. He entered the ER room with a tool bag swinging from one hand. He wore tan shorts and a button-up Hawaiian shirt. His flip flops clapped against his feet walking across the speckled linoleum floor. The specialist used a Makita battery-powered drill that he pulled out of a Makita zippered tool bag to bore a hole in Teddy's skull. The whole time the specialist was working, he was whistling the tune from Gilligan's Island. After he was finished, he said, "That should be that."

The entire procedure took less than ten minutes.

Thanks to a tool that you can buy at Home Depot and a guy in a Hawaiian shirt and flip flops, they say Teddy has a chance of regaining consciousness someday. Maybe. The actual words vary from "a chance" to "a slim chance" to "Lanaya, have you thought about what he would have wanted done in the event of…?"

The ghost of Mom is still playing the broken accordion machine that's pumping air in and out of Teddy's lungs. I need to work on saying goodbye to her. Right now, we're a forever fractured family. From this moment on, I need to stop looking for the magical and start focusing on the practical.

I know what you're thinking: This isn't how stories are supposed to start. And you're right. Let me start somewhere else.

"The Specific Gravity of Airplanes and Houses"

Teddy wasn't the first AFO (Anachronistic Falling Objects) casualty, not by a longshot. Objects were falling out of the air and maiming and killing people way before Teddy was struck.

Even back in the 1900s, there were incidents, but those were more like parts coming off planes, rainstorms of fish, dead bats raining down, or golf balls coming from the clouds. And that's weird, but not as weird as everything that started coming down two years ago.

Our AFOs don't need dark clouds or abnormal weather patterns. It could be a perfectly clear sky through which a mint-condition Edison record player could plummet toward you at terminal speed. That record player could make a crater in your yard, your car, or your body. Imagine a single object coming all that way (who knows how far) just for you. There's something grossly intimate about that.

That Edison player isn't just some hypothetical item I came up with. It's the same object that didn't quite kill Uncle Teddy's neighbor, Bob Thorn, but did paralyze him. Bob will tell you that it saved him. But don't listen to Bob. He's only saying what people say who live through things they shouldn't have. He's only trying to save his sanity with magical thinking.

In the last two years, there have been tens of thousands of AFO injuries and deaths in America, and only in America. That's weird, right?

Teddy started calling it a "gross domestic problem" because that's how Teddy dealt with things that were horrible: by twisting them.

We're all trying to deal with things.

Churches are packed with people trying to deal. Deacons will tell you that the objects mean something, that God is sparing the church. They won't bring up the fact that some of the other places that anachronistic falling objects haven't hit are libraries, Subway sandwich restaurants, and porn shops (how amazing is it that a physical place for porn is still around?). Those preachers will glaze over the fact that schools get hit all the time, because nobody wants to think of children being unfairly punished. Physical school won't be around for long anyway; they've been going out of fashion since the early 2000s.

Scientists point to the destruction of the ozone layer as the cause of the AFOs.

None of these AFO incidents make sense. But we're sensible creatures. We need to make sense of things. We need to feel safe somewhere. Our brain wants to put everything into nice, sensical boxes and make a coherent story out of random pieces.

I'm safe at church.

I'm safe at the library.

I'm safe at the porn shop.

I'm not safe at school.

Where is safe? Who is safe? What is safe?

The Bermuda Triangle Theory is currently en vogue on the internet. But the BT Theory doesn't explain the cavalry horse in full regalia (with rider intact) that fell out of a cloud into the middle of a Yankee's game, taking out the second baseman. It doesn't account for the apple tree that fell, inverted, onto a car driving across the Golden Gate Bridge yesterday. Nobody has ever transatlantic-ed an apple tree, have they? The Bermuda

Triangle doesn't explain the stained-glass window that hit my A&P professor in the head last week. That window still had the surrounding pieces of a house attached to it. Helmet or no helmet, Mr. Gordon is still in the ICU because of it.

Everybody's afraid.

We've always been afraid, but never of something so unpredictable, so unexplainable.

You know how you hear things on the news and it's real, but not really real? That's how the AFOs were to all of us when they first started, just these pockets of weird. Then Mom was hit by one, and the weird became the unthinkable. Mom was only forty-five years old when the propeller blade that the investigator's report called "a disembodied projectile from a P-51 Mustang" killed her.

"What? A Mustang? A car part?" I'd said, even though it didn't matter what took her from us; the horrible part was that nothing was bringing her back.

"No," said Uncle Teddy, "it's a plane prop from World War II. I don't know how the hell that's possible, but that's what they're saying." For the first time, Teddy didn't have anything else to add.

"Why would they say that?" I couldn't stop crying. I couldn't stop trying to make sense. If I could just make sense. If I could just make it all mean something.

"I don't," Teddy sighed, "know," with one hand to his forehead.

It was the first time I saw Teddy cry. His crying made me cry harder. Once I finally stopped crying, I haven't been able to cry since. You know what stops tears? Facts.

The report of the incident said the propeller blade missed Mom's carotid artery but severed her subclavian. The subclavian artery runs on the underside of your collarbone. Even in a parking lot filled with people trying to help, Mom lost enough blood for her heart to stop beating in front of the Safeway on Halsey through that severed artery. I can't bring myself to go to Safeway anymore. I wasn't even there in that parking lot, but I dream about it all the time.

I dream I'm trying to clamp off a burst garden hose with a pair of pliers in the middle of the street.

I dream I'm trying to hold a smashed plum together on a train ride to nowhere.

I still see Mom before the incident, after the incident. When I'm asleep. When I'm awake.

I used to follow women who look like Mom (like me) into supermarkets and stare at them while pretending to check a cantaloupe or a watermelon for ripeness. But I was only checking those ladies' likeness to Mom. Maybe those women were only pretending to check the fruit in their hands too. Maybe we're all just pretending.

Sometimes it feels nice to pretend.

But it's not easy to pretend when you're constantly bombarded by another incident: the rusted typeset letter L from an antique printing press that lodged itself in the skull of a father of twins getting out of his car in Minnesota, the still-writhing giant octopus that flattened a bicyclist on Hathorne Street, the SS Waratah ship (after disappearing in 1909) that took a nosedive into a horse barn in southern Washington state last month.

So, I've decided that it doesn't matter where these AFOs are coming from. Whether it's a curse or a wormhole or the apocalypse, it doesn't matter. We can't save ourselves. We can't stop gravity. Everything gets pulled down. Everything.

You know the one thing that we might have a chance at controlling?

Bleeding.

If you do it right, if you train hard enough, it's entirely practical, it's totally doable.

After Mom died, I kept looking up different ways to stop a hemorrhage.

The tourniquet is the most obvious blood stoppage, but Mom was bleeding out from the subclavian artery (under her collarbone), and you just can't tie off an entire chest. If I came across a hemorrhaging subclavian in the hospital parking lot, or any street corner between here and home, or anywhere just anywhere, I'd dam it up. I'd pack it full. I'd put all my body weight on top of it. That's something I could do if given the chance. I'd push rolls of cloth into the wound until it either stopped bleeding or there was no more blood to lose or I was hit by an AFO myself and bled out.

I carry a pack of medic field tourniquets and packing gauze on me. You can buy them on Amazon. You should get some. You know the packets of powder that are supposed to cauterize wounds? Amazon has those too.

Even if you don't want to help anybody, how does that old saying go? "The life you save could be your own."

You should prepare to at least save your own ass.

I'm trying to be ready for the next falling thing. I don't care where it comes from. I only care where it lands. And if I seem obsessed, that's okay. If you're reading this, you're probably obsessed too. You're probably afraid as much as I am.

They say that "practice makes tourniquets" and "nobody ever did anything without keeping the arteries intact" and "hypervigilance is the mother of insomnia." Actually, I'm probably the only one who says those things. I don't know. The insomnia worries me though. Your head's not right when you don't sleep.

I do sleep sometimes, not a lot, but sometimes. Like I said, I even dream.

I dream of trying to tape up multiple pinholes in a water balloon the size of a person's liver.

I dream of never-ending mud squishing between the fingers of my fists.

I dream of giant concrete dams breaking apart around me.

In the dam dream, the concrete always starts out solid and pristine. A small pillar of water knocks a chunk out of the dam onto the ground. Then another chunk pops, shooting past my face. And another. There's water everywhere, but there are also all these random items at my feet. In the dream, I start shoving the items into the growing number of gushing holes. None of the items make sense. I cram baby shoes, balls of yarn, and entire pizzas into the holes where the water is gushing. The escaping water is brown with algae and silt. It doesn't feel like water. It's thick and sticky, staining my clothing.

I realize that I'm standing in a canal, and the canal is flooding around me. I pick up floating pairs of pants and socks and start plugging them into the bursting dam. I pick up throw pillows and pages of paperback books and push them into the spouting holes. The thick water is rising around me, and the holes keep coming. I reach down and pull at a shirt sleeve with ruffles at the cuffs. It's my mom's favorite shirt that I'm pulling up. The shirt is always the heaviest in the dream because Mom's still wearing it, floating on her back in the now waist-high water.

There is black pudding coming out of her neck and shoulder. I try to stop it, but the pudding oozes through my fingers. I want to throw up and cry and lay on my back and float with her, but I can't; I have to keep plugging the holes. Mom opens her mouth and coughs up a tennis ball. With the hand I'm not using to tamp the pudding, I grab the tennis ball and force it in another hole in the dam. Mom opens her mouth, and a plum falls out; it bobs in the water and starts to sink. She opens her mouth, and brown water shoots into the air. There's a sound coming out of Mom like a jet engine. I can feel the dam shaking. Mom is pointing with one arm to the sky high above us. Her eyes are not her eyes.

The ruined dam is quivering, buzzing, humming to explode around us. I look up and see elephants careening out of a blazing orange sun. The elephants are spinning and trumpeting. I can't stop looking at them. You can't look away from what's never supposed to happen. The tusks are coming down. The rough, grey skin is almost upon us. The elephants. And that's when I wake up coughing and screaming.

I don't know how many times I've had this dream.

"Lanaya, are you all right?" says Rachel.

She is Teddy's day nurse. Rachel is wearing blue scrubs with white daisies on them, and she's next to Teddy's bed. There's a binder in her arms. Yesterday she wore black scrubs with white pieces of chalk on them. I wonder how many scrubs she owns.

The broken accordion machine is still wheezing out its rhythm without Mom's ghost needing to play it. Mom can't be here. The image of Mom is still stuck in the dream. The cardiac machine is beeping. Teddy isn't talking. This is Teddy's new norm.

I nod. "Yeah, I'm fine. I just startled myself. Thanks, Rachel." Knowing the hospital nurses by name is never a good thing.

If places where people die aren't safe, then hospitals should be the least safe.

"You should go home," Rachel says. "Take a shower, get some rest. I promise we'll call you if anything changes."

I look at Teddy, the tube coming out of his mouth, his chest rising with the compression of the broken accordion.

"Yeah," I say. "Yeah." I know Rachel's right. I know I need to do all the things she mentioned, but I'm afraid for Teddy. I'm afraid for myself. I'm afraid to fall asleep again, and I'm afraid of not ever sleeping well.

In the movies, houses only fall on witches. In real life, houses fall on other houses. A house fell on Teddy's house. That's why he's here. Nobody is safe anymore, anywhere. This is Teddy's new norm. This is everybody's new norm.

"Looking for Elephants"

Before leaving Teddy's hospital room, I check my hair and face in the en suite bathroom. I always try to keep the lights dim, but this bathroom is either all black or all light. I flick the switch. The fluorescents are harsh. The mirror is harshest. I don't look quite as bad as Teddy, but that's only because my face isn't as loose-fleshy as his, I have less goo at the corners of my eyes, and I'm upright.

I wash off whatever makeup is left off my face. I run a brush from my fanny pack through my hair. I gather my hair up with both hands and pull it tight behind my head. My facial structure is so pronounced that I'm convinced I know exactly what my skull must look like. Would anybody still say I look like Mom? I can't remember the last time I've eaten a full meal. I can't remember what real hunger is. I let my hair fall back down. It almost hides the way my ears stick out. Because of my ears, I've never been a fan of putting my hair back. But now, nobody does tight ponies. You can't wear a helmet with your hair tied back.

I put the palm of my hand on the back of Uncle Teddy's knuckles and squeeze. I slide my helmet back on while exiting his hospital room.

Downstairs in the lobby, I sprint from the hospital entryway to the idling Uber. There's a concrete canopy covering my entire journey from the hospital doors to the car door, but that doesn't matter. I run anyway. You run everywhere. Even when you don't think you should run, you should still run. I open the rear car door and slide in, and I'm enclosed inside the vehicle in seconds flat. Everything done outside is done in seconds.

There's a starred crack on the driver's side of the windshield. Every windshield that hasn't been retro treated is cracked. Even some of the retrofits are cracked.

"Abdul?" I ask, knowing it's Abdul because my phone has already told me "Abdul" would be arriving in this particular vehicle. It's habit to double-check.

"Yes, I am Abdul," he waves back.

Abdul is wearing a yellow construction helmet. The top of the helmet still grazes the ceiling of the car even though his seat looks like it's as low as it can go. "You are Lanaya?" he says as he puts the car into gear.

"Yes."

I adjust my fanny pack so the car seat belt will fit snug around my waist. Most people don't carry purses or bulky backpacks anymore. They're just one more accessory you don't need to weigh you down when you're scanning the sky, running for a car, trying to dodge an inbound cow with milkmaid and stool in tow. That milkmaid bit isn't a joke. I wish those kinds of object-triplets were just jokes.

"How's your day so far, Abdul?" I don't really want to talk, but I also don't want to appear like I don't want to talk.

"It is good. It is a clear day. I mean…I am sorry. You must have someone in there at the hospital. I am sorry for you and your person."

"Thank you. It's fine," I say, even though it isn't.

"My mother. She had a stroke last month."

"I'm sorry." And I am sorry, but it's also a relief to hear of somebody with a tragedy other than another AFO incident. A natural death. "She is…"

"Gone. Yes."

"I'm sorry."

"Yes, you said that. Thank you. I had not seen her in years."

"Were you able to see her before she…"

"No. She was still in Sudan. With the airlines…well, you know."

I do know. It turns out that we can't fly high enough to avoid a falling object. No matter how high our planes go, the objects fall from higher, with the same velocity, like they are falling from space. I know that's not possible. When the impossible happens anyway, we call it fact all the same. When more people started dying in AFO-related airplane incidents than the number that used to die in car wrecks, most people stopped flying unless absolutely necessary. With so many people not flying, it stopped being very profitable to own an airline.

The Concorde—the same plane that was retired in the early 2000s because it was too expensive to maintain after it crashed, and everyone onboard died, and everybody else thought, maybe I won't do that—is now the only passenger plane still in the air. The same reasons that made it obsolete in a thriving airline market—flying at nearly twice the speed of sound and tens of thousands of dollars for a one-way ticket—are the same reasons that it's back in the air today.

It's funny how facts feel safe, even when they are improbable. It's interesting how knowing something holds power.

But even the Concordes don't fly much anymore, because it turns out most people don't really need to fly. Except for people like Abdul: landlock refugees. And landlocks can't usually afford to fly back home, wherever home is.

"In the end times, everything will be ultimate irony." Didn't Jesus or Dante or Carlin say something like that?

I feel like I just missed something Abdul is saying.

"I'm sorry?"

"Excuse me, Lanaya. You do say that you are sorry a very lot. You do not need to be sorry for anything on this ride."

"Maybe."

"Maybe? Maybe how? Maybe another planet will fall from the sky tomorrow. There is no more room for maybes in our world."

"Maybe."

"Ahhh," Abdul laughs loudly, "I like you, Lanaya. You let no one off easy. Not even me, your humble Uber driver." He smiles in the rearview mirror.

I'm impressed by the ease that Abdul holds a conversation while continuously scanning the sky, the traffic, his rear and sideview mirrors. His head is a constant motion of swivels and sways. Not so much a bobblehead, but more like a graceful, smooth perpetual-motion-machine, like all the attention a bird pays its surroundings without all the stiff and choppy tics.

The blackness of the back of Abdul's neck shines in the sunlight coming through the side window. For a minute, while watching him drive, I forget about everything that's ever fallen. How strange it is that being an Uber driver has become a heroic profession, only taken up by the steeliest of nerves. For this short ride home, I'm in trained hands. I'm at ease. I'm safe.

I. Am. An. Idiot.

At first, I don't understand what's happening. I know the windshield was intact just seconds ago, and now there's a hole in it. I know that we were moving, and now we've abruptly stopped. I know that the inside of Abdul's car was almost spotless, and now there are blood spots and feathers everywhere. We've probably hit something. Or, more probably, something's hit us. I know that my stomach and chest and neck are throbbing, that the side of my head feels warm and my knees don't feel right.

Abdul's head is tilted toward his chest. He is half-moaning, half-hissing in the driver's seat. I take my seatbelt off and lean between the front seats. There is blood at the side of Abdul's mouth. The hollow of his stomach is a pool of crimson and torn fabric. The steering wheel is bent firmly against his thighs. There are giant wings trembling in the passenger seat, a bloody trail over the center console.

I've thought of a million scenarios that could lead to me needing to stop someone from hemorrhaging out, but I wasn't ready for the eagle's barely breathing body lying on the passenger side floorboard. I hadn't planned on making sure I wasn't too dizzy to stand after opening the back door of an Uber driver's car. Hadn't planned to fling open the front door and be faced with such destruction.

I'd planned on saying, "Don't worry, I've trained for this," to someone in need. But when I say, "Don't worry, I've trained for this," now, it doesn't sound as reassuring as I'd hoped it would.

I don't tell Abdul that I have no real-world experience as I pull the remnants of his shirt up to his chest to fully reveal his abdomen. We both look down at the mess of what was his stomach. He looks away quickly and squeezes his eyes shut.

It wasn't supposed to be like this. I wasn't supposed to want to puke everywhere and run away and start screaming.

I focus on the mantra my first-aid instructor said years ago: "I hate the sight of blood too. That's why I cover it up."

I need to cover this up.

I reach into my fanny pack for a potential covering. I rip open the top and start pulling gauze out of the plastic pouch like a magician's never-ending hanky, and I shove the gauze into Abdul's gaping stomach. He's trying to push my arms away, trying to fight my hands.

"Trust me," I say. "Trust me." I keep pulling and pushing until I realize there's more blood than gauze.

"Stay away, I said," Abdul hisses. He must be hypovolemic already because he's weaker by the second. His brain must be oxygen-deprived.

"I'm trying to save you. Please!" I take out another pack of gauze and keep pulling out and pushing in. "You want to live, don't you?"

Abdul doesn't say anything. His eyes glaze around me. He starts making a constant shrieking sound.

I hadn't considered how surviving a wound like Abdul's might feel worse than dying.

I grab another package and pack and pack and pack.

When I'm out of gauze, I place my now-red hands on the gauze bits bunching out of Abdul's stomach. A single car drives by without stopping or honking or slowing. You can't stop, not when every second of being outside is bloated with consequences. The eagle on the floorboard lies still.

The sky is still clear. Abdul has stopped shrieking and is breathing rapidly. There are sirens far away in the distance, or maybe not. Maybe they're just my imagination. Maybe it's an ambulance from the 1980s, somewhere miles above us, plummeting down.

I close my eyes and picture Teddy dancing on top of the kitchen table, trying to make me laugh at my fifteenth birthday party. There's no accordion machine. I picture Mom smiling. There's no dam breaking. I think of Abdul's mom dying naturally, how nice that must have been. I match my breath to Abdul's breath until he stops breathing. I hold my breath.

I wait for the next falling thing...for every falling thing, for the entire world to drop out from under us. The sun is a burnt-out orange hole in the sky. I'm staring directly into the burnout, looking for the out-of-this, looking for the elephants, waiting for the next crack to give way.

On My Final Day,

I Had an Explonut

by Ameerah Sanders

Holy shit, today is the day. I get to fucking die. Couldn't ask for a better day really. The sun is shining, only 120 degrees! What a lucky lady I am. I pull out my planner. Each activity has been meticulously picked out. As I slather SPF 500, as is government regulation, I smile gazing at the bright silver walls of the high-rise from my kitchen window. Gosh, just in time. That high-rise raised my rent sky-high. But do I got to worry about it? No! Because today I'm fucking dying.

Donning my sun hat, as is government regulation, I hop into my rideshare. The driver is super friendly, as are the other seven people on board.

"Hey! Happy death day!" the driver says.

"How did you know?!" I squeal.

"You got that glow!" he shakes his head." Mine isn't for another ten years."

"Oh, you'll get there, buddy."

"Either that, or the New Plague will get me!"

We all laugh. The new plague is active all the way in the Arctic and Scandinavia. Nowhere near us!

I chat with the lady beside me, off to her fourth job: RV shit-tank dumper. It's awful, but she makes rent every month, so can't complain, right?

I'm dropped off second. I paid the second most; thought I'd splurge for the big day.

I step foot on the nicest sidewalk I've seen in awhile. What more would you expect from the Diamond District? I get in line at the checkpoint. When it's my turn, I lift up my skirt and reveal my ass. It is branded with my citizenship ID mark, as per government regulation.

"Have a lovely day, miss," the officer says as he smacks my verified American ass.

"Thank you, sir!"

My ass undulates with mortal fever. It's time for a donut.

I allotted time for this. The wait is usually two hours. Never bothered to do it before because I had work, but now, who gives a shit? These donuts have been famous for three whole months. They only stay edible for five minutes after purchase. So you have five minutes to take your picture, edit it, upload it, and then eat your donut before it explodes. Stomach acid neutralizes the explosive. It's fun!

A few times in line, I hear the familiar firecracker sound of the donuts exploding. Sometimes people just let them explode for the fun of it. The donuts cost fifty dollars. I've already decided to eat mine. When I finally get it, I shove it all the way in my mouth just like I saw online one time. "THE MOST EFFICIENT WAY TO EAT YOUR EXPLONUT!" was the video title. It tastes like the donuts my mom gets from the store, but the danger makes them extra special.

My next and final stop is the botanical gardens. To get in, you have to forfeit your genetic code to the nation's database, as is government regulation. Take it! I won't be using it much longer. One quick swab and I'm in.

"Enjoy, miss!" the clerk smiles.

I smile as well. We both know they already have my DNA. I don't know how. Maybe that terms and conditions I signed when I signed up for that cat food delivery service?

The botanical garden holds some of the last species of plants. I rush to go see the oregano. No one has had oregano in thirty-five years! Italy is distraught.

I don't get to see the oregano. It's like the Mona Lisa of plants. Well, can't expect this world to give you gifts even on your death day.

I make a point of being early for my death. If you miss your appointment, you are sniped where you stand, and that is not a good look.

My friends and family can't make it. They're all working, but they wish me the best. This is more for my family anyway. Spoiler alert: I have an autoimmune disorder, and keeping me alive isn't financially viable anymore. This way my body can be exchanged for five whole years of free class-C energy. If they keep the lights off during the day, that is enough energy for every night for those five years. What a deal!

I walk to the death center from the botanical garden. The closer I get, the more I meet people who are also ending it all today. We don't speak. Mostly nervous smiles all around. I see a couple holding hands. Aw, double death day! That's what us romantics call a murder-suicide.

We are all gathered in front of a large, clear building. The structure looks see-through. We see the high-rises behind it clearly. They built it this way so people wouldn't be reminded about it all the time. Some people find this custom "barbaric," but hey, no more sixteen-hour shifts and communal bathrooms. I'll take it. Life in the cloud is much better. Worth dying for. You get to live an ideal life forever. Heaven. Literal heaven. And it only costs my physical body.

A door opens, revealing a bright white rectangle in the middle of the high-rises. We all enter.

The room is wide and cavernous. Once the last of us enter, the door shuts, and we are surrounded by never-ending whiteness. Then, the ceiling suddenly goes pink.

"Your families thank you," a female voice says.

"You're welcome," we say. It starts the sequence.

The last thing I see is the couple kissing. The last thing I feel is warmth. The last thing I think: It's not my problem anymore.

www.ingramcontent.com/pod-product-compliance
Lightning Source LLC
Chambersburg PA
CBHW030544310726
48979CB00010B/2022/J

* 9 7 8 1 7 3 4 5 4 9 7 0 6 *